A Goofy Guide to Penguins

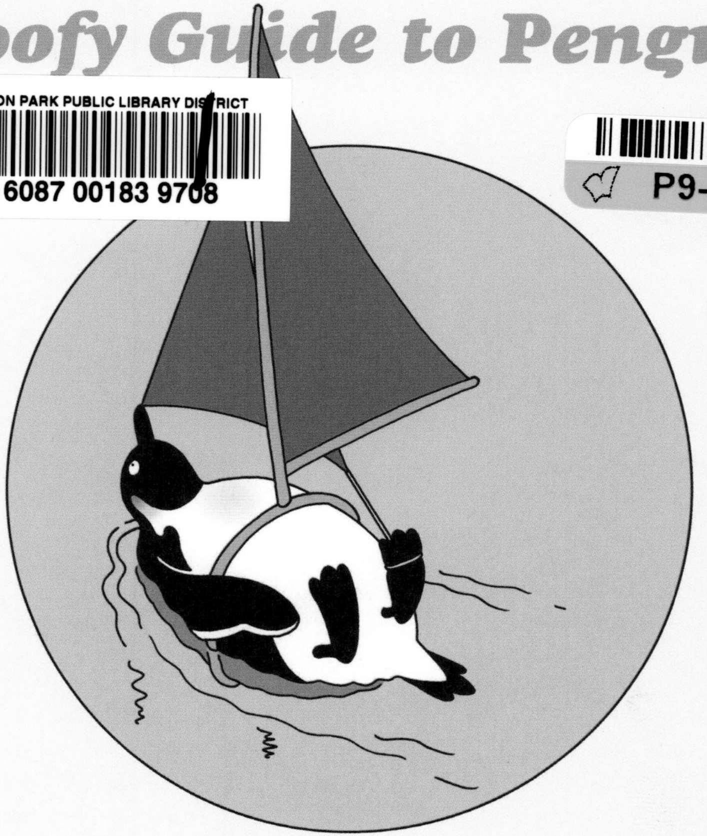

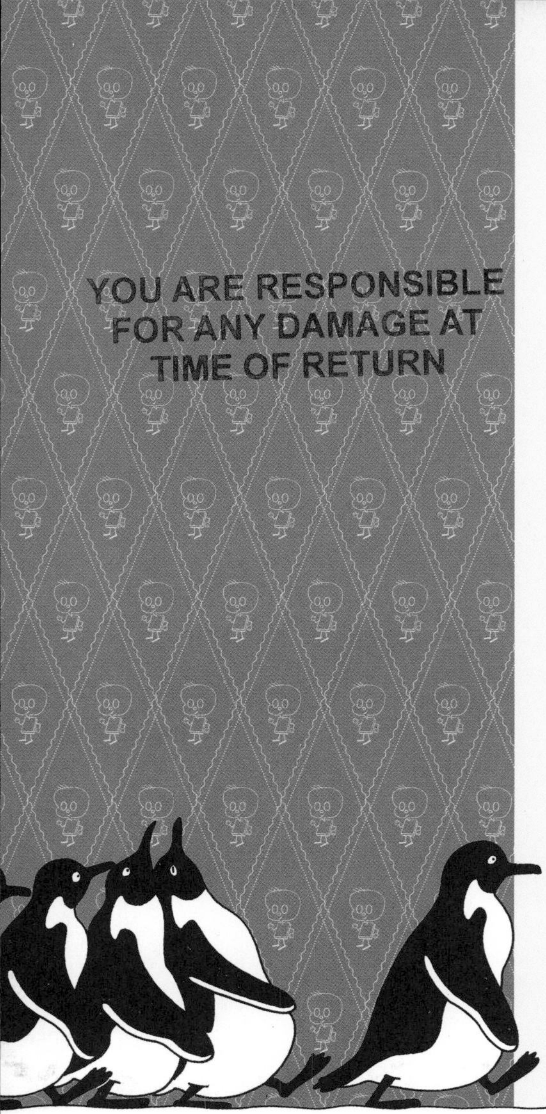

A TOON BOOK BY

Jean-Luc Coudray & Philippe Coudray

For Margaret Webb, a true animal lover

Editorial Director & Designer: FRANÇOISE MOULY

PHILIPPE COUDRAY'S artwork was drawn in India ink and colored digitally.

A TOON Book™ © 2016 Jean-Luc Coudray, Philippe Coudray & TOON Books®, an imprint of RAW Junior, LLC, 27 Greene Street, New York, NY 10013. Original French text and art ©2013 Jean-Luc Coudray, Philippe Coudray & La Boîte à Bulles. All rights reserved.

No part of this book may be used or reproduced in any manner whatsoever without written permission except in the case of brief quotations embodied in critical articles and reviews. TOON Graphics™, TOON Books®, LITTLE LIT® and TOON Into Reading!™ are trademarks of RAW Junior, LLC. All our books are Smyth Sewn (the highest library-quality binding available) and printed with soy-based inks on acid-free, woodfree paper harvested from responsible sources. Printed in China by C&C Offset Printing. Distributed to the trade by Consortium Book Sales; orders (800) 283-3572; orderentry@perseusbooks.com; www.cbsd.com. Library of Congress Cataloging-in-Publication Data: Coudray, Jean-Luc, 1960-   A goofy guide to penguins : a TOON book / by Jean-Luc Coudray & Philippe Coudray.   pages cm   Summary: "A collection of humorous short two-panel comic strips featuring the fanciful antics of penguins, which are portrayed doing everything from trying to warm themselves with radiators to putting on stylish hats to tell each other apart."–Provided by publisher. ISBN 978-1-935179-96-2 (hardcover : alk. paper)   1. Graphic novels. [1. Graphic novels. 2. Penguins--Fiction. 3. Humorous stories.] I. Coudray, Philippe, illustrator. II. Title.   PZ7.7.C678Go 2016   741.5'6944--dc23   2015030595

ISBN: 978-1-935179-96-2 (hardcover)

16 17 18 19 20 21 C&C 10 9 8 7 6 5 4 3 2 1

www.TOON-BOOKS.com

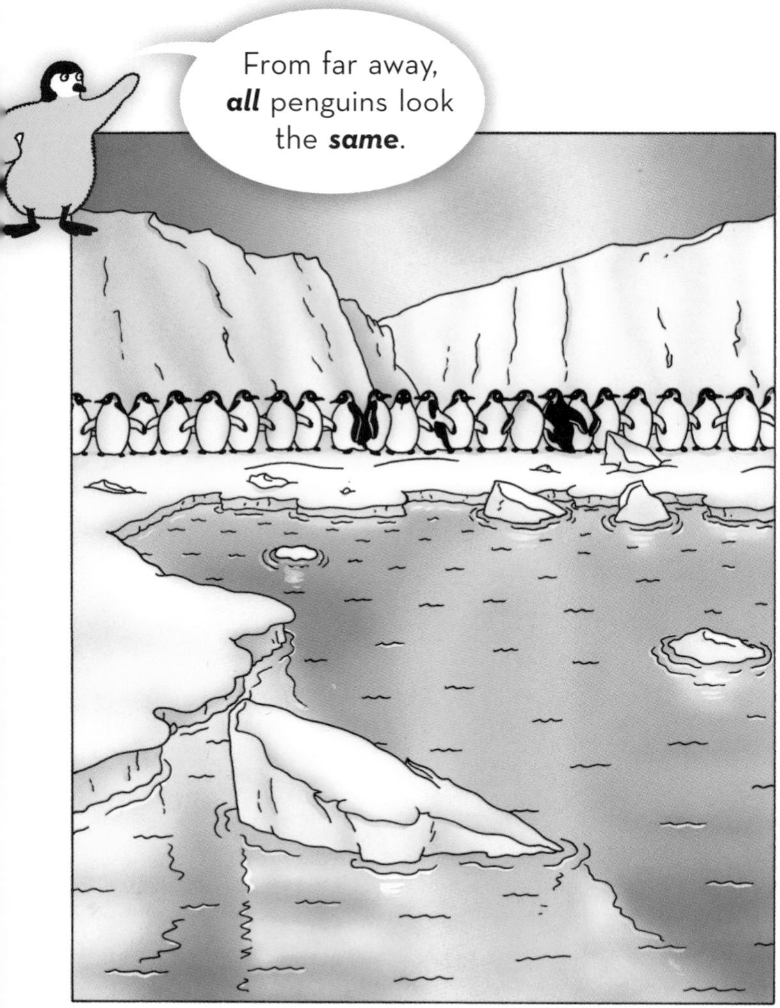
From far away, ***all*** penguins look the ***same***.

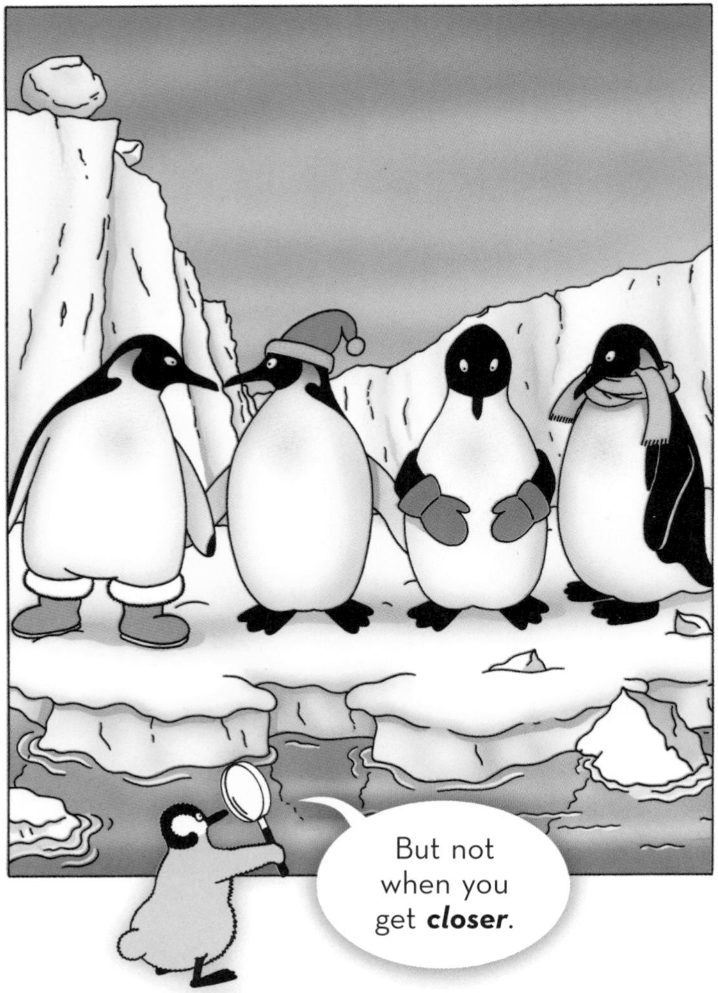
But not when you get ***closer***.

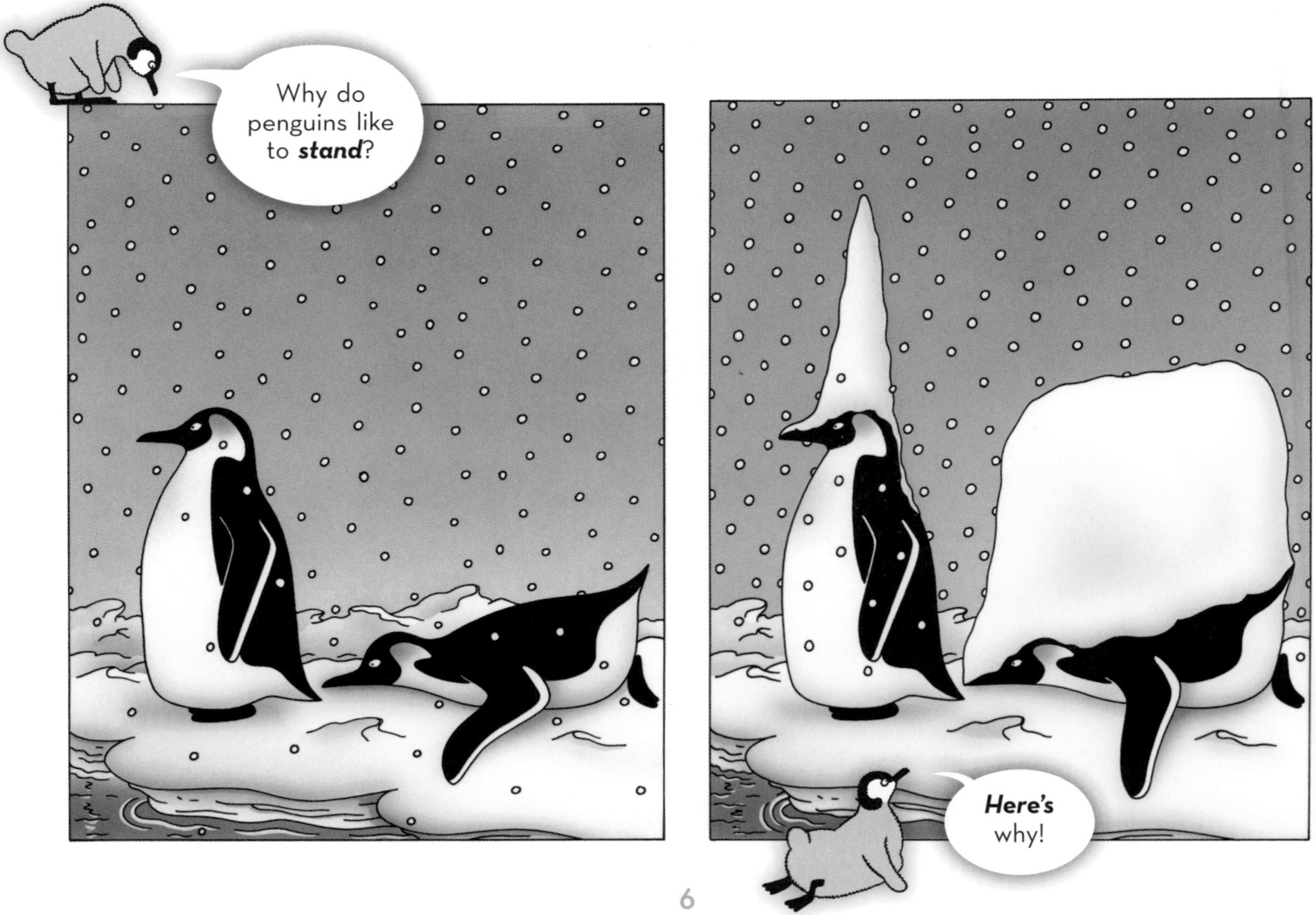
Why do penguins like to ***stand***?
Here's why!

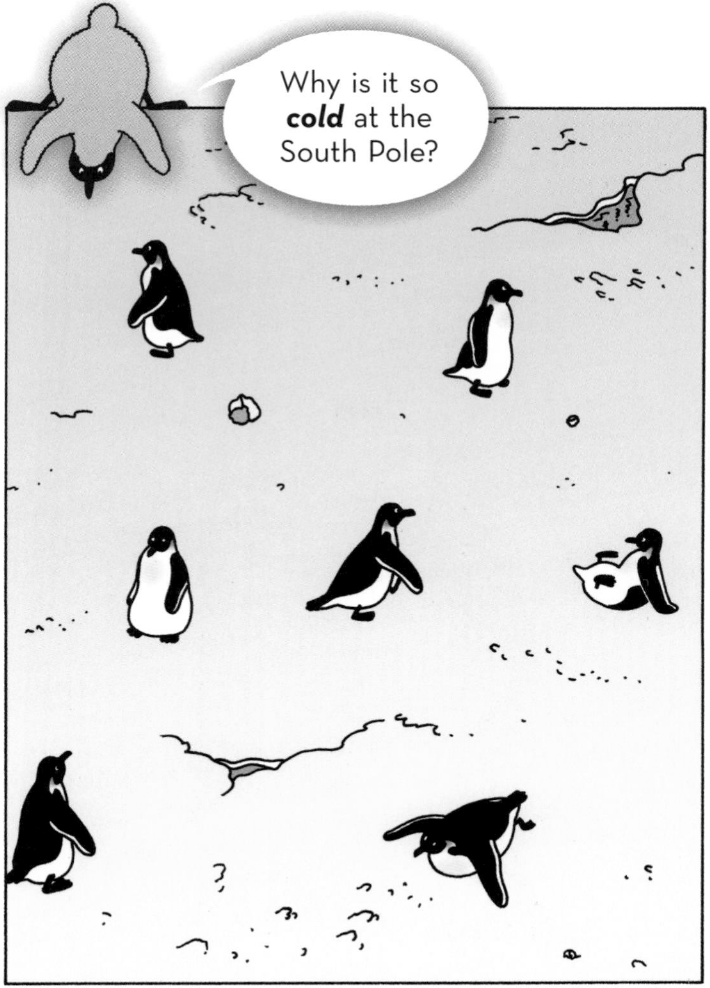
Why is it so **cold** at the South Pole?

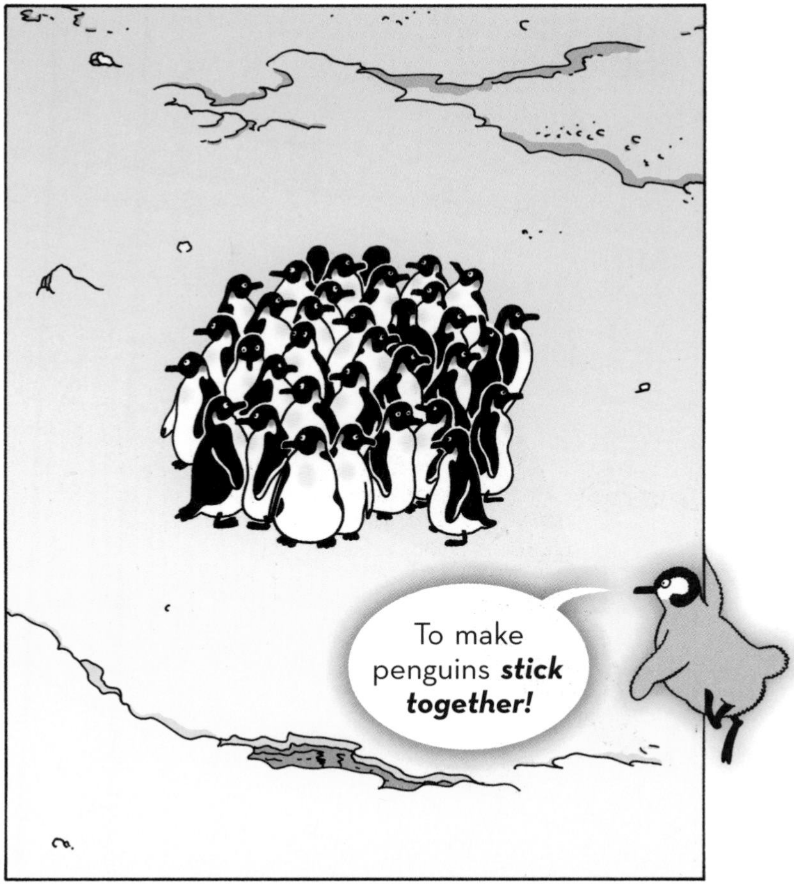
To make penguins **stick together!**

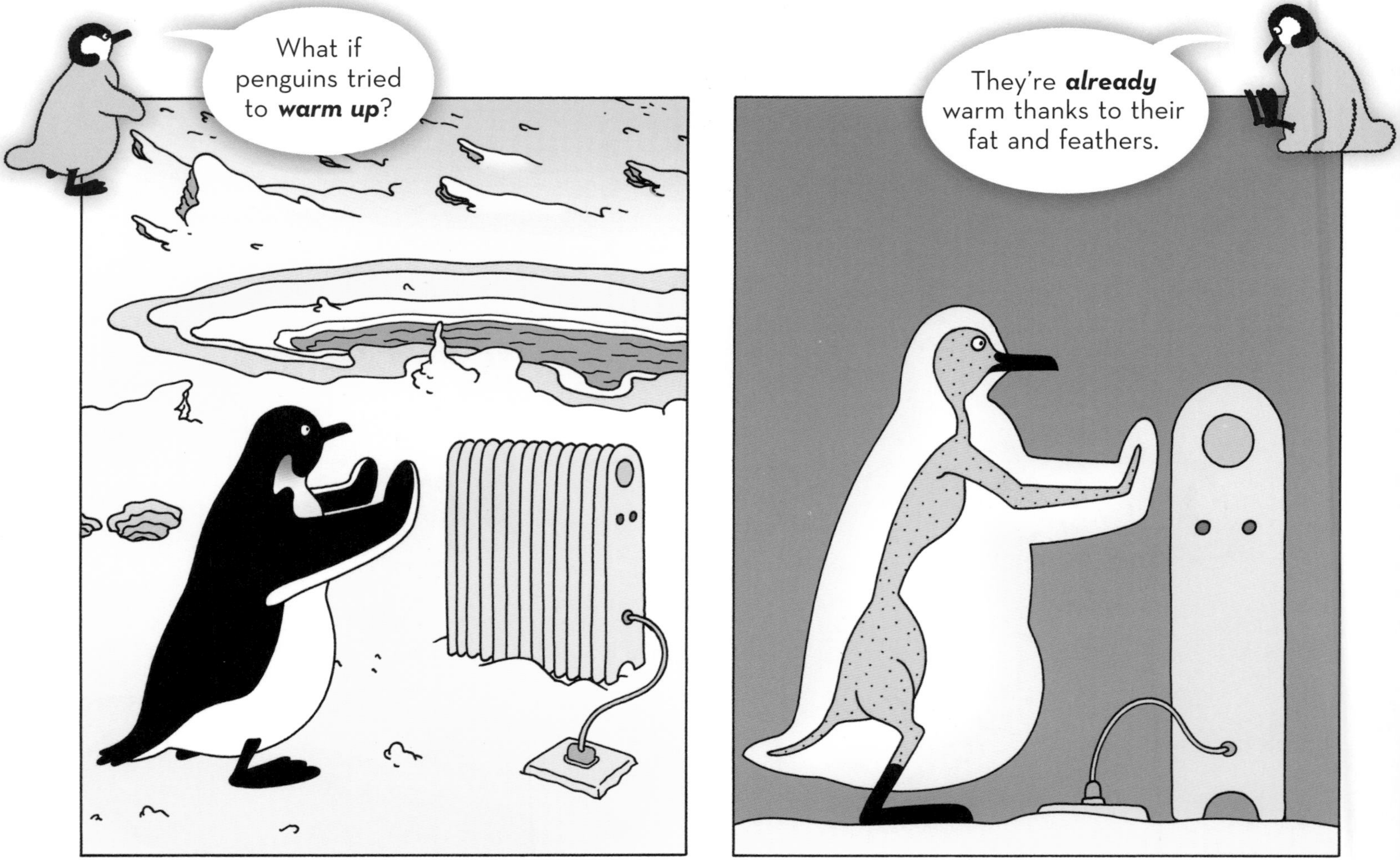
What if penguins tried to **warm up**?
They're ***already*** warm thanks to their fat and feathers.

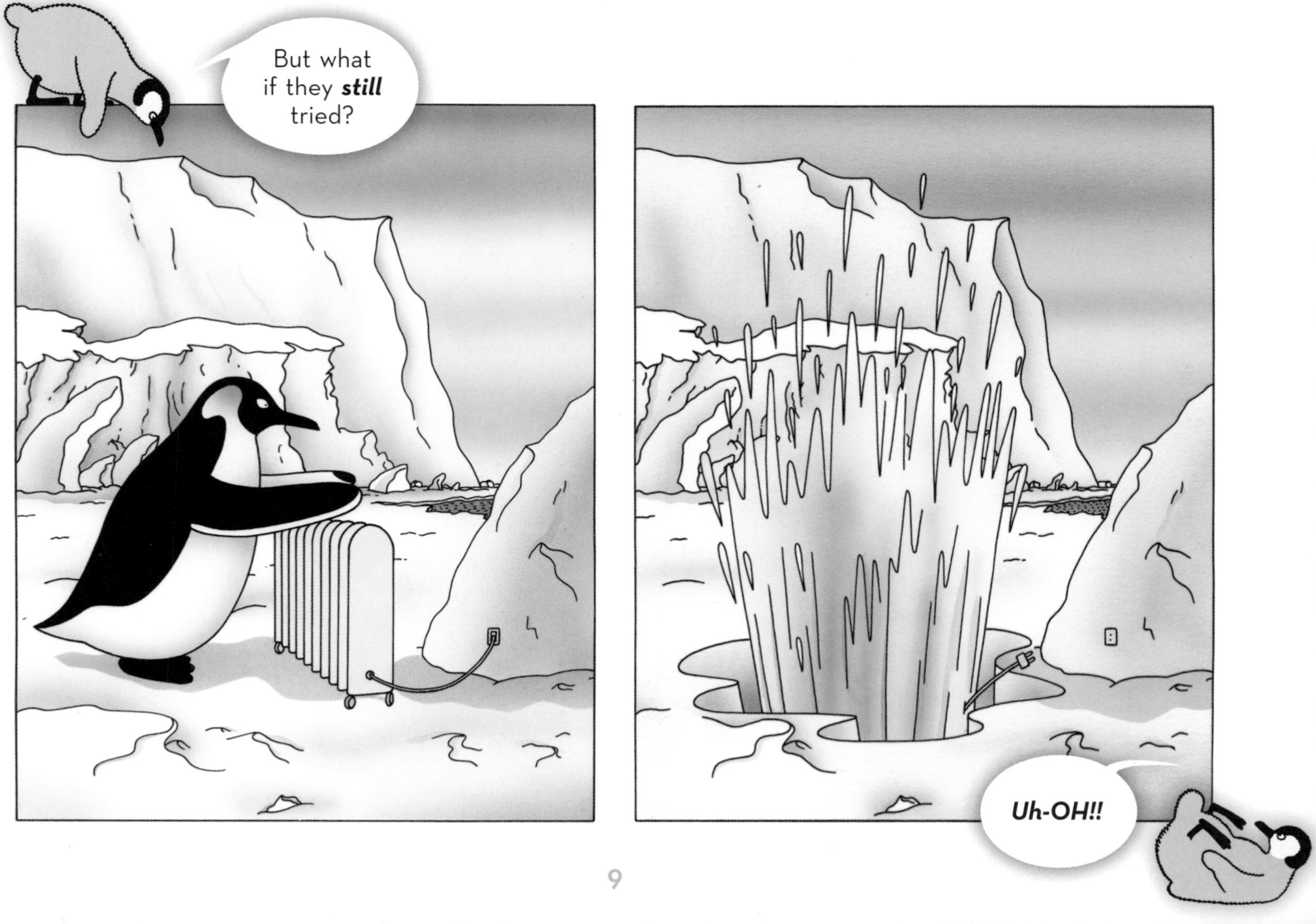
But what if they ***still*** tried?
Uh-OH!!

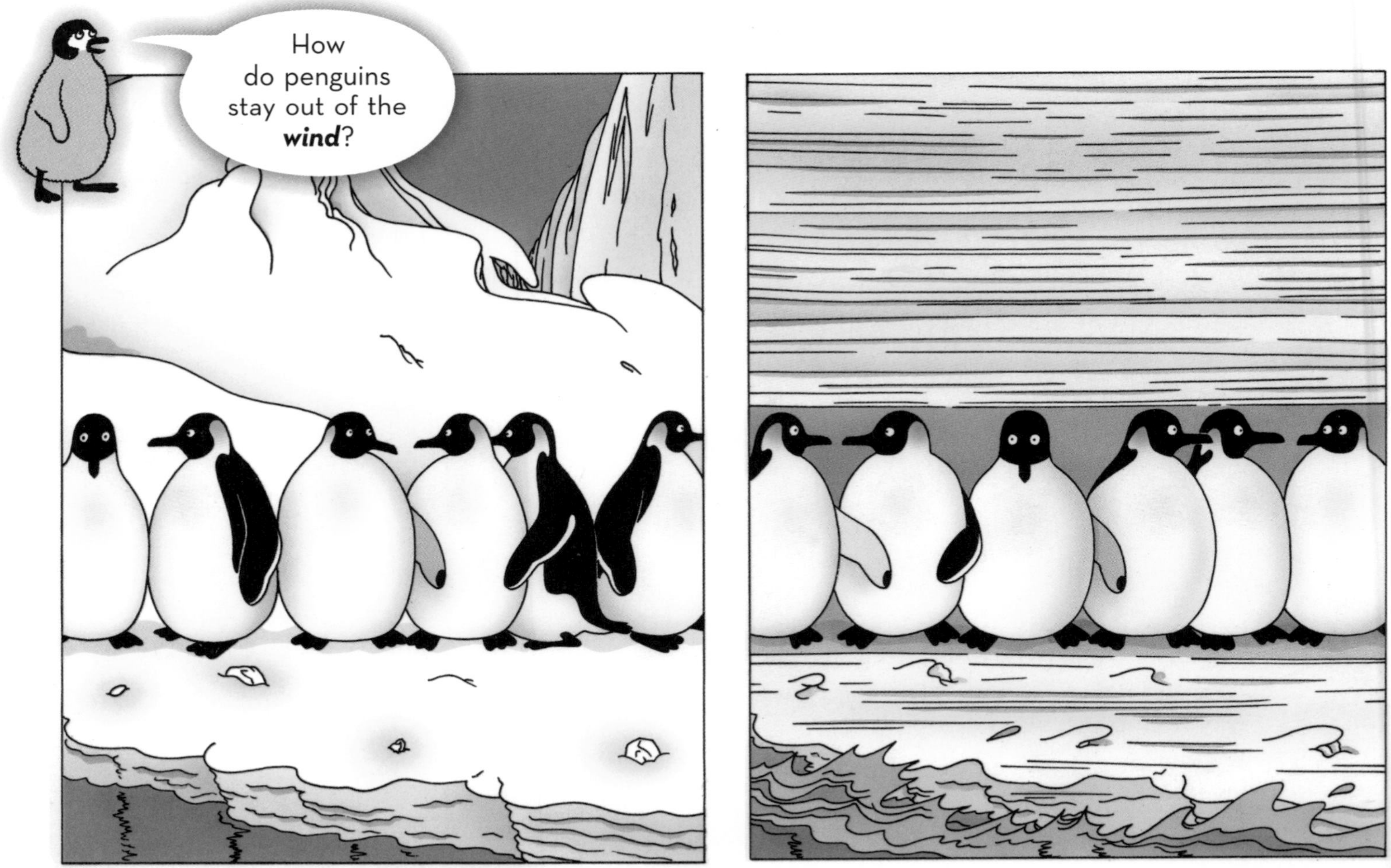
How do penguins stay out of the **wind**?

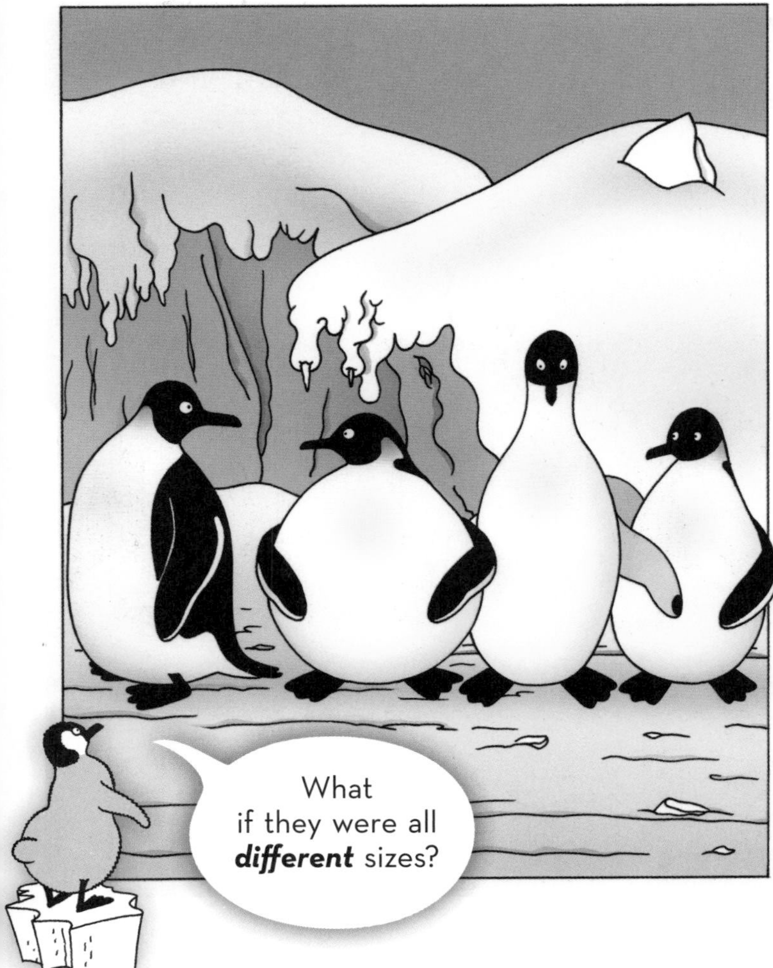
What
if they were all
different sizes?

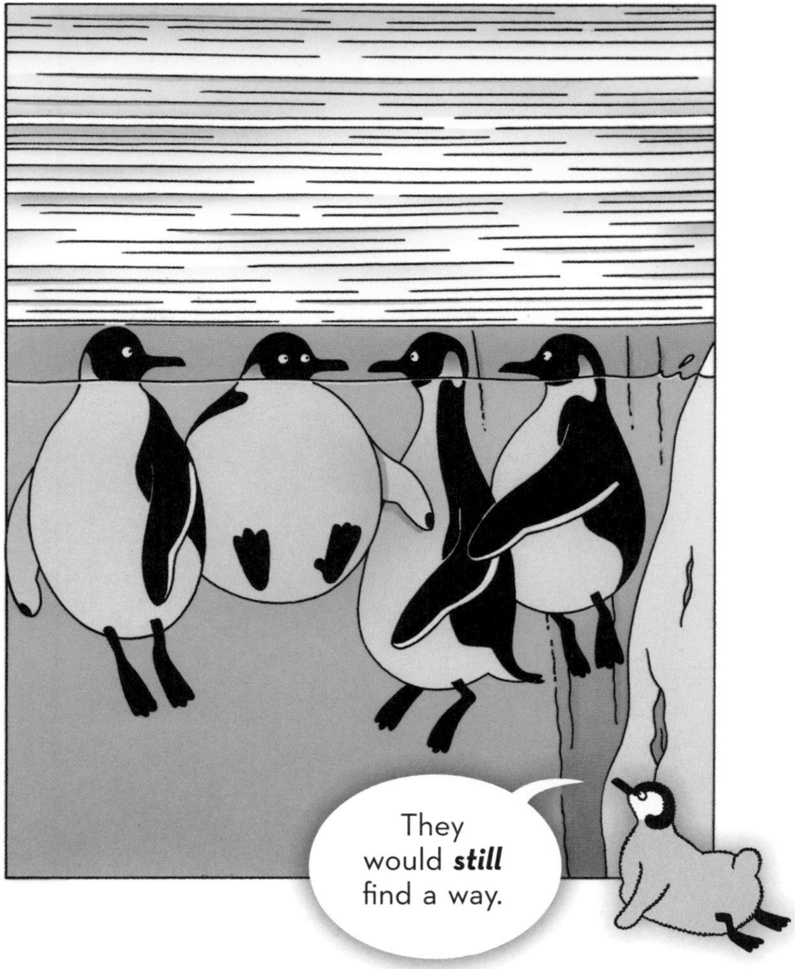
They
would ***still***
find a way.

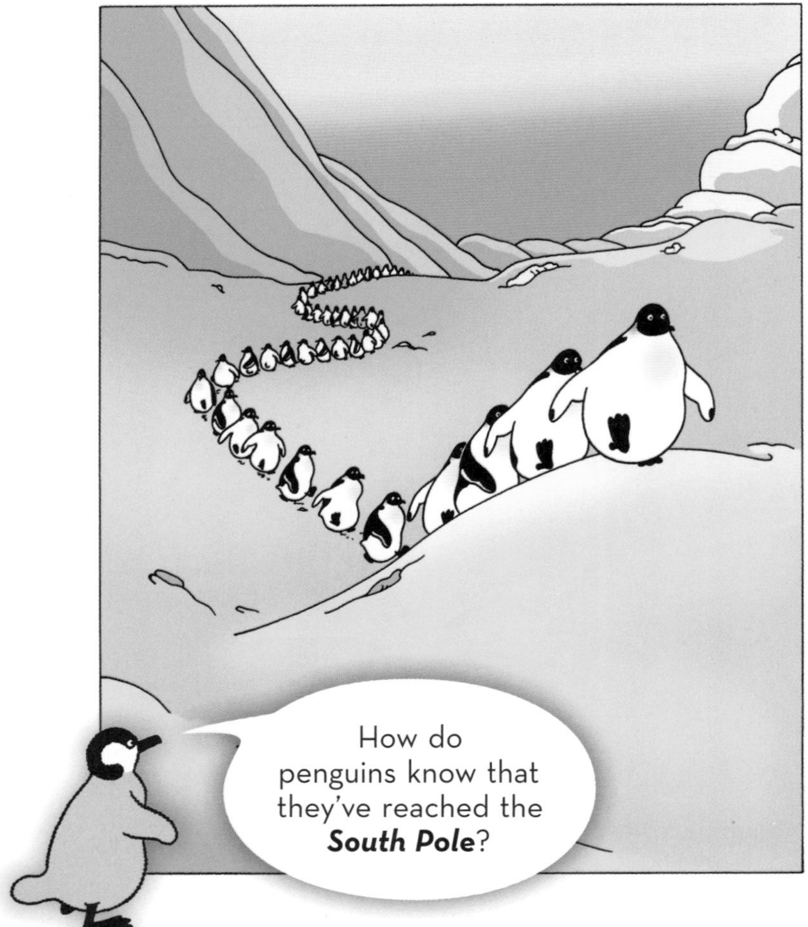
How do penguins know that they've reached the **South Pole**?

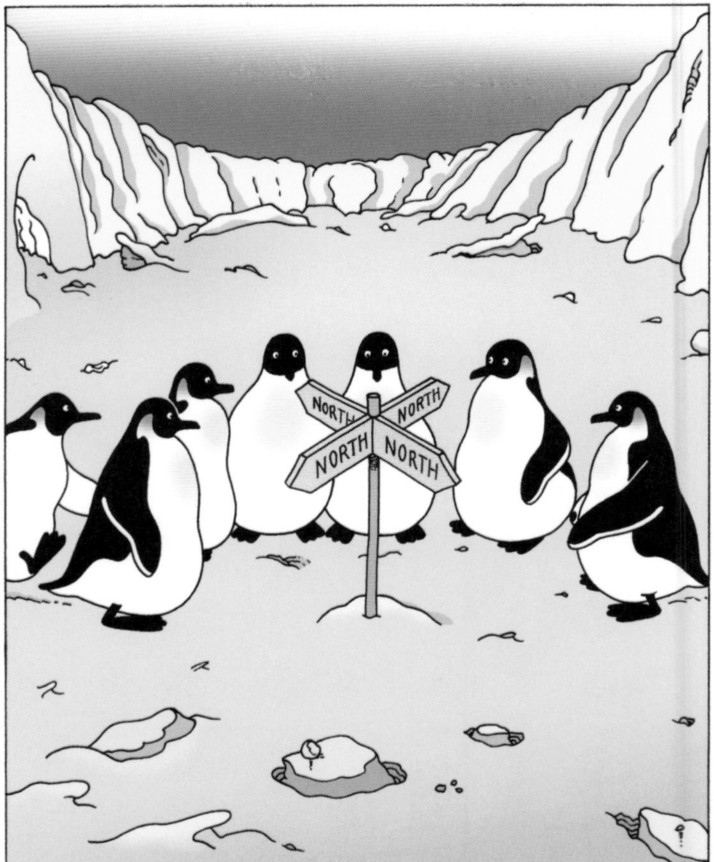
NORTH
NORTH
NORTH
NORTH

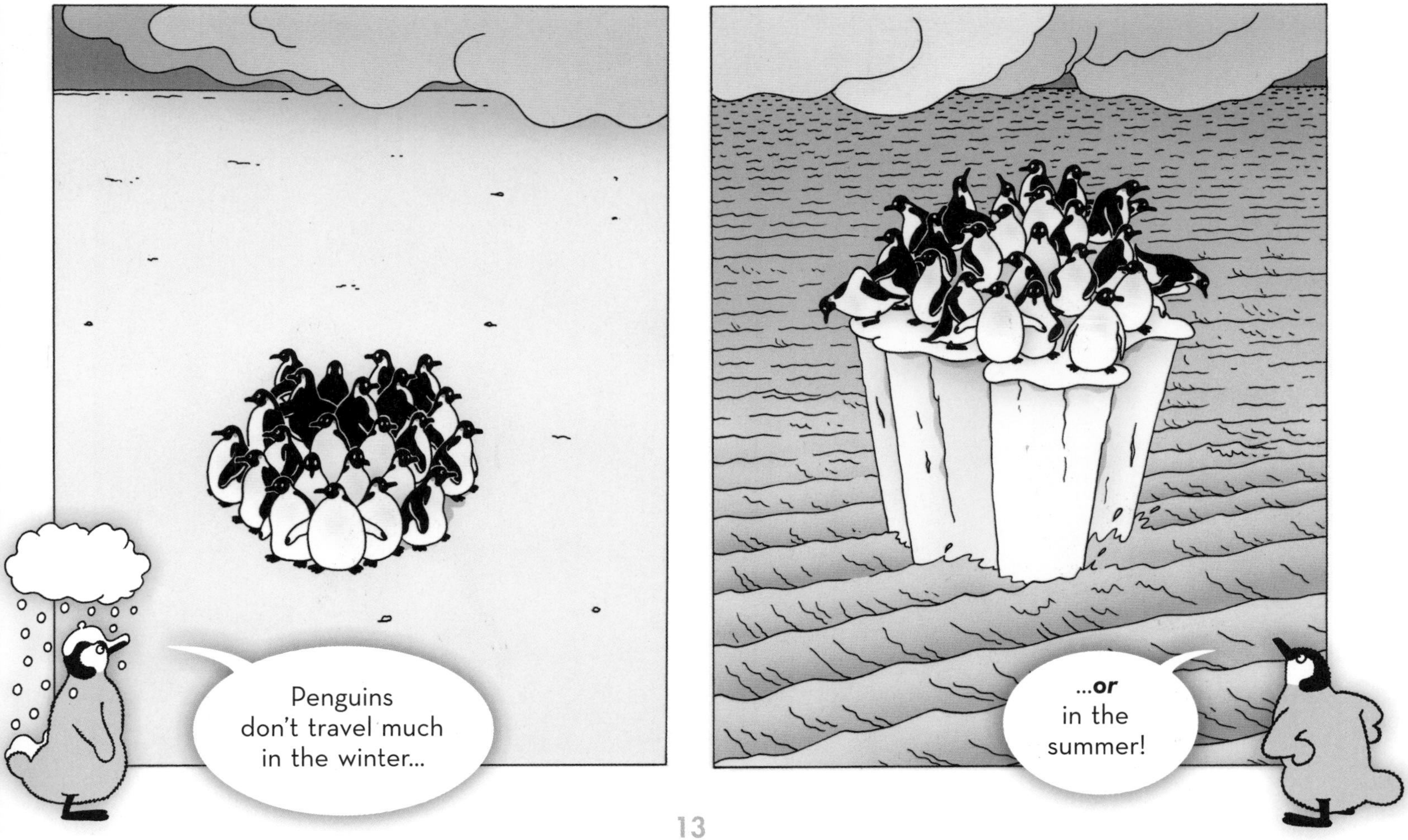
Penguins don't travel much in the winter...
...**or** in the summer!

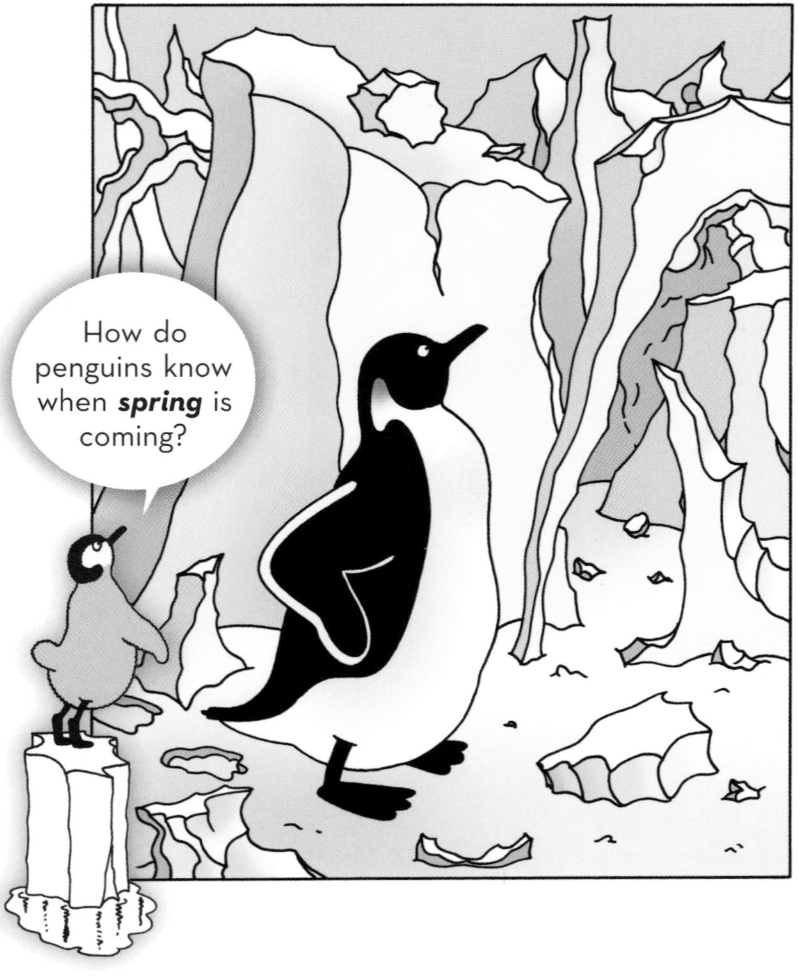
How do penguins know when **spring** is coming?

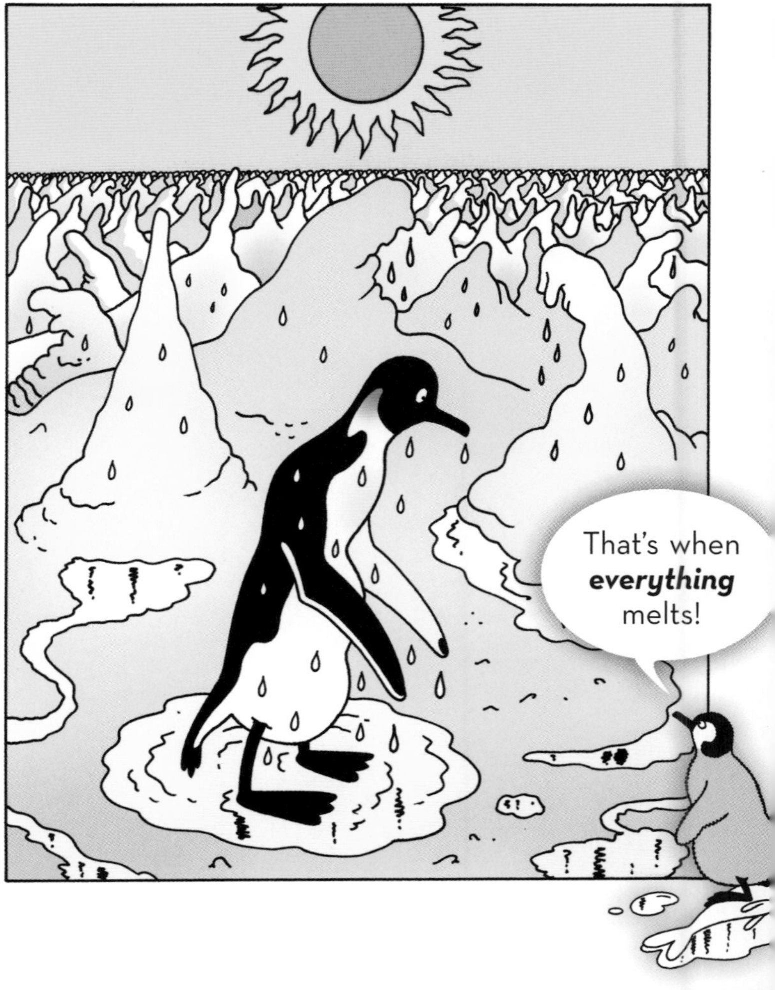
That's when **everything** melts!

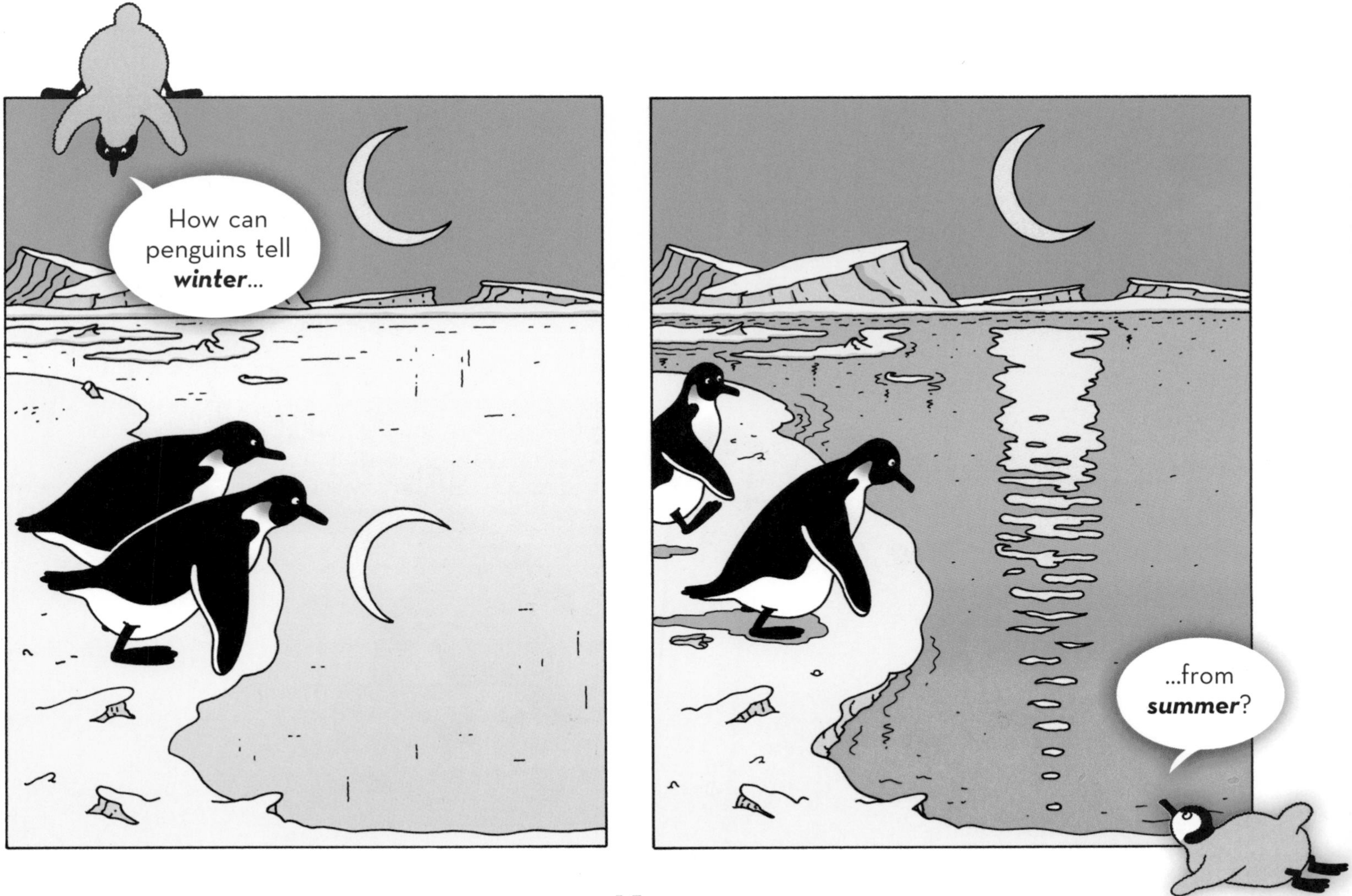
How can penguins tell **winter**...
...from **summer**?

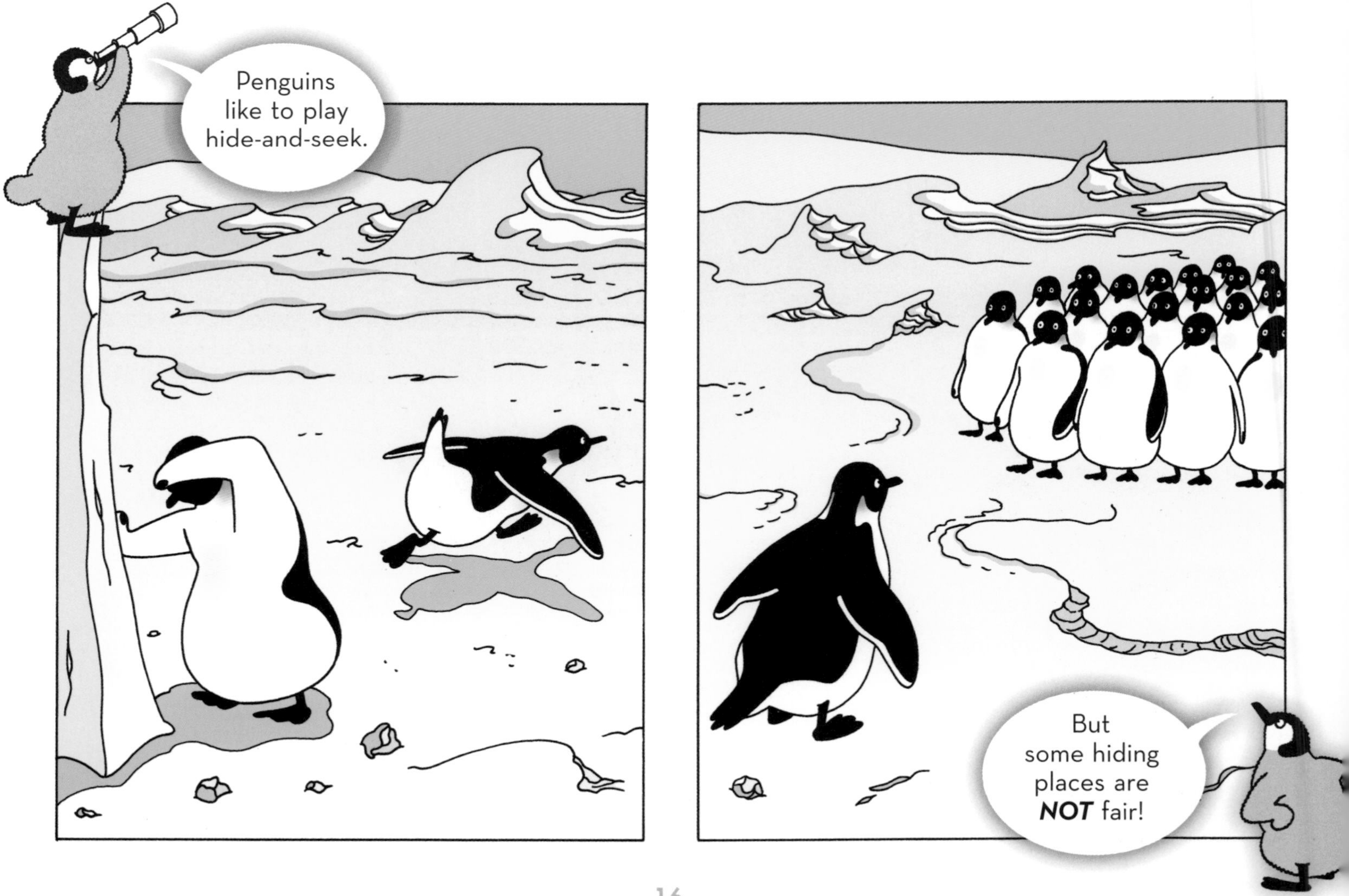
Penguins like to play hide-and-seek.
But some hiding places are ***NOT*** fair!

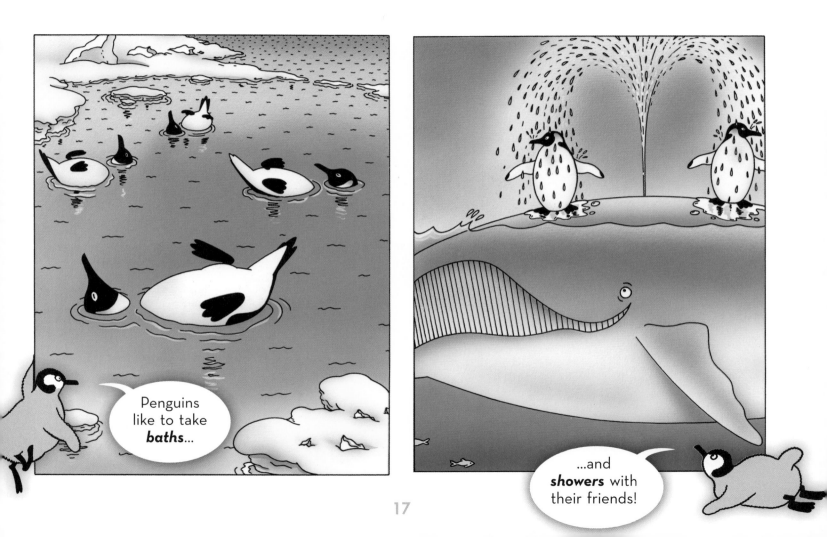

Penguins like to take **baths**...

...and **showers** with their friends!

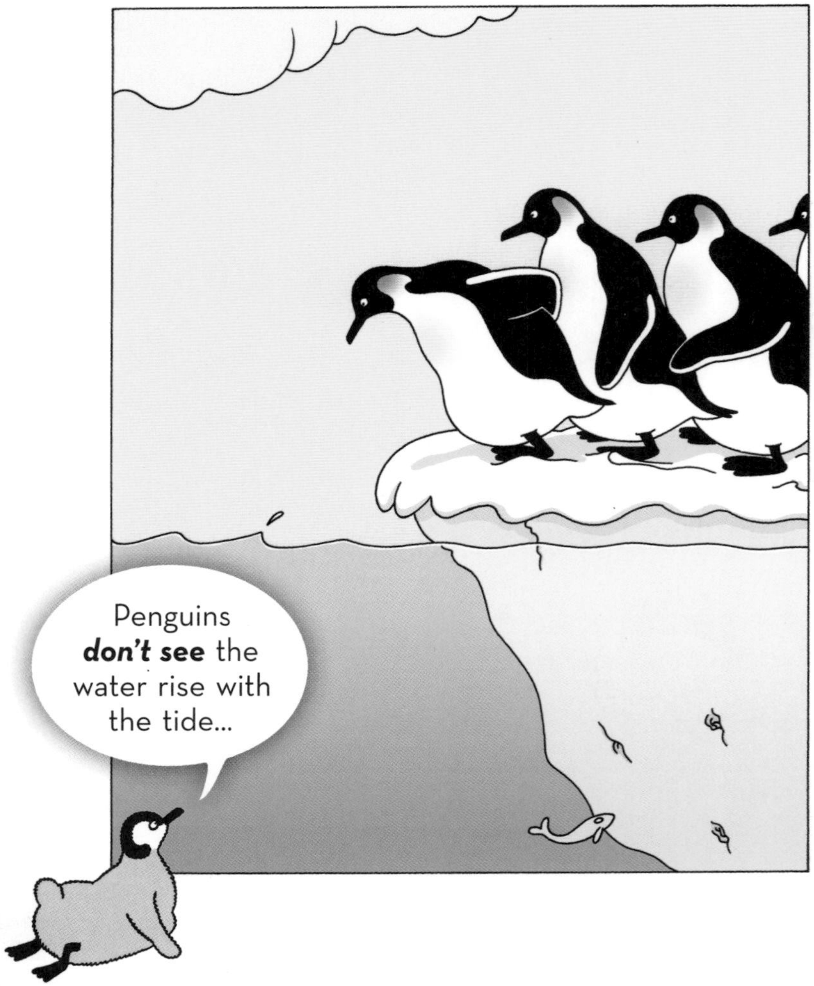
Penguins **don't see** the water rise with the tide...

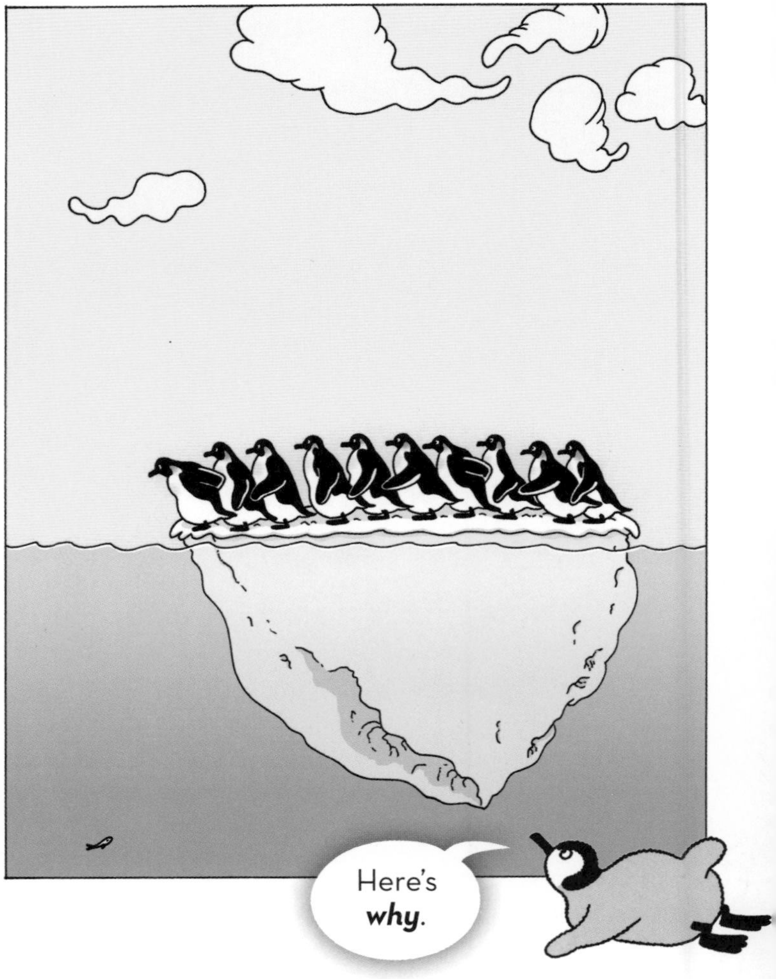
Here's **why**.

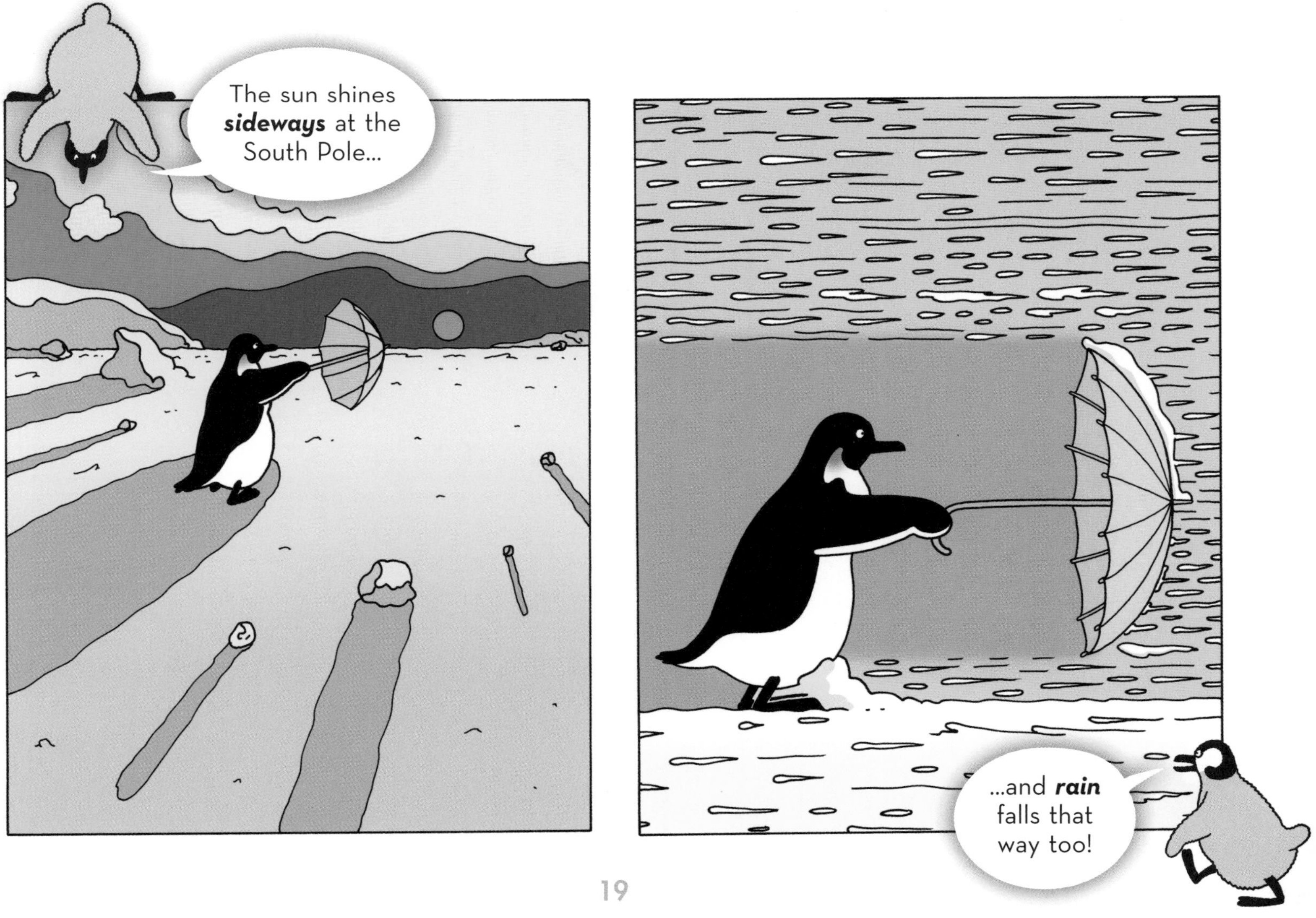
The sun shines **sideways** at the South Pole...
...and **rain** falls that way too!

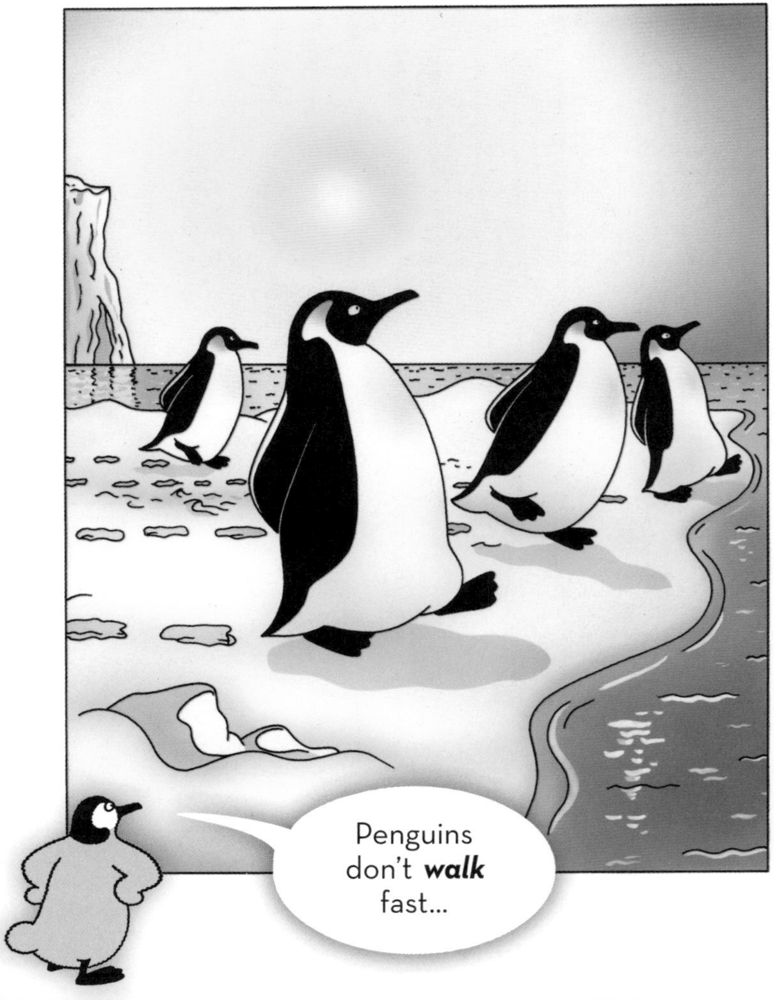
Penguins don't **walk** fast...

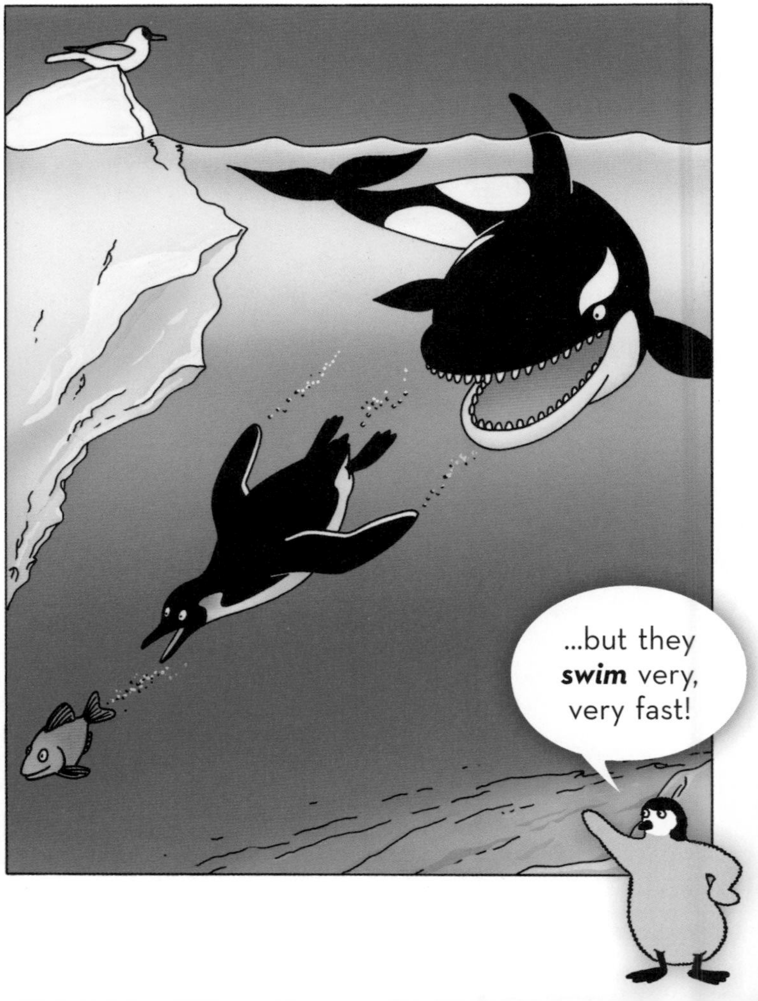
...but they **swim** very, very fast!

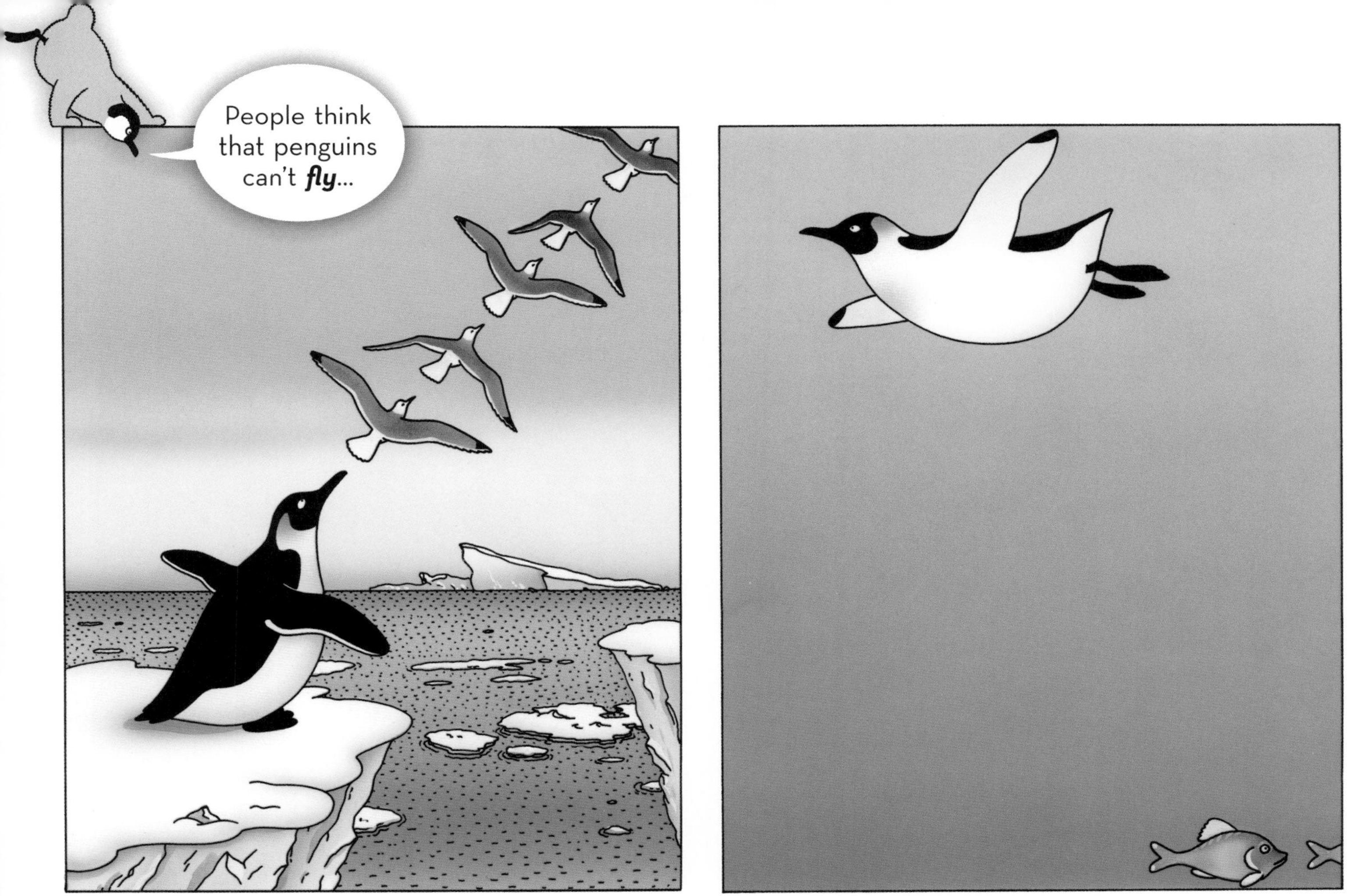
People think that penguins can't ***fly***...

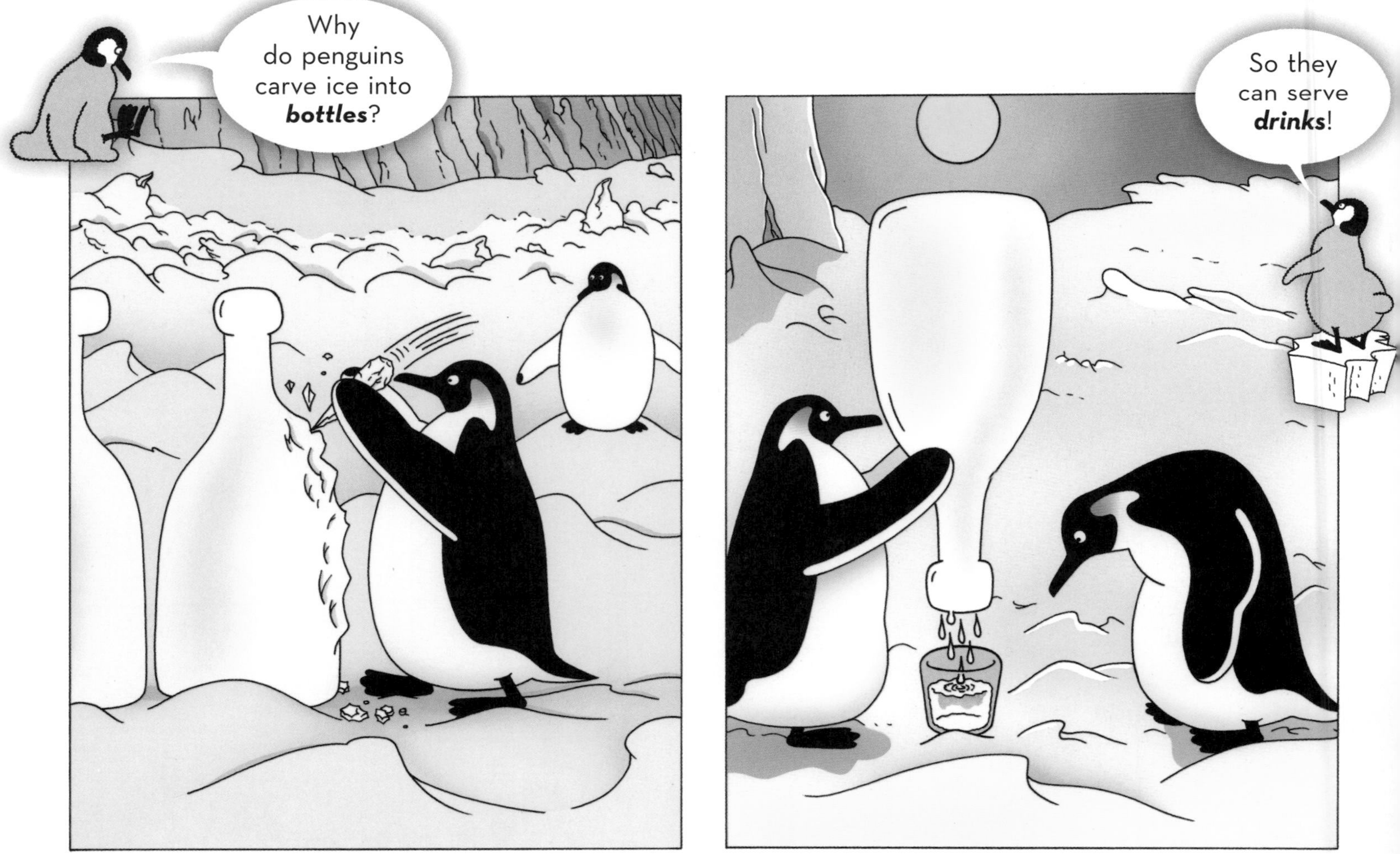
Why do penguins carve ice into ***bottles***?
So they can serve ***drinks***!

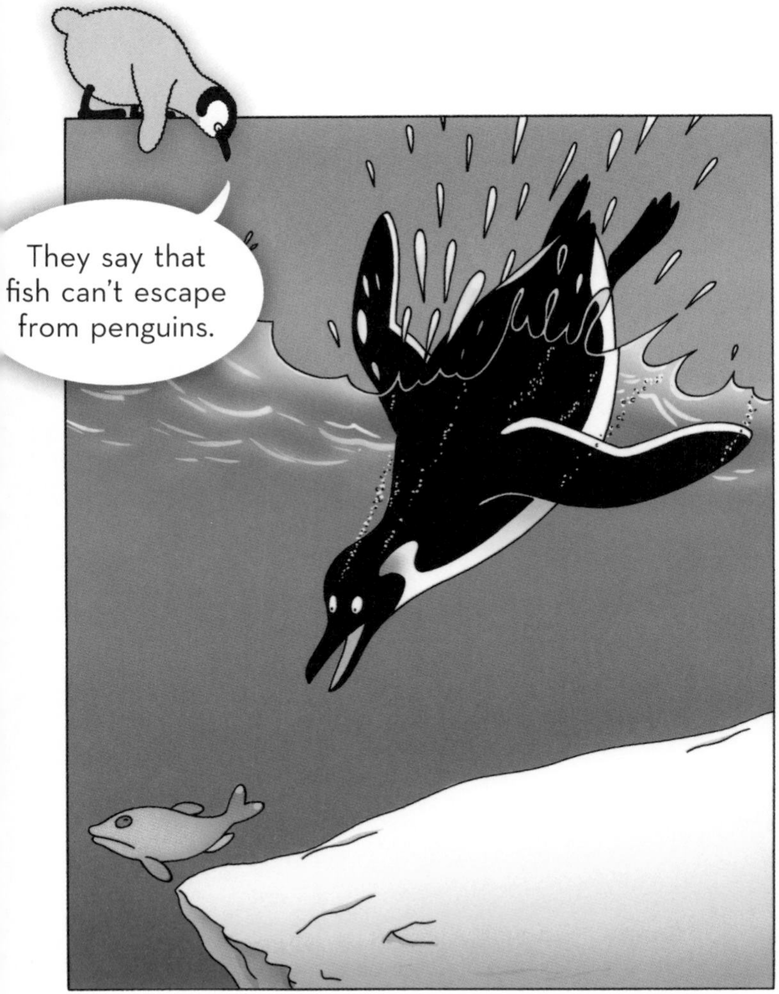
They say that fish can't escape from penguins.

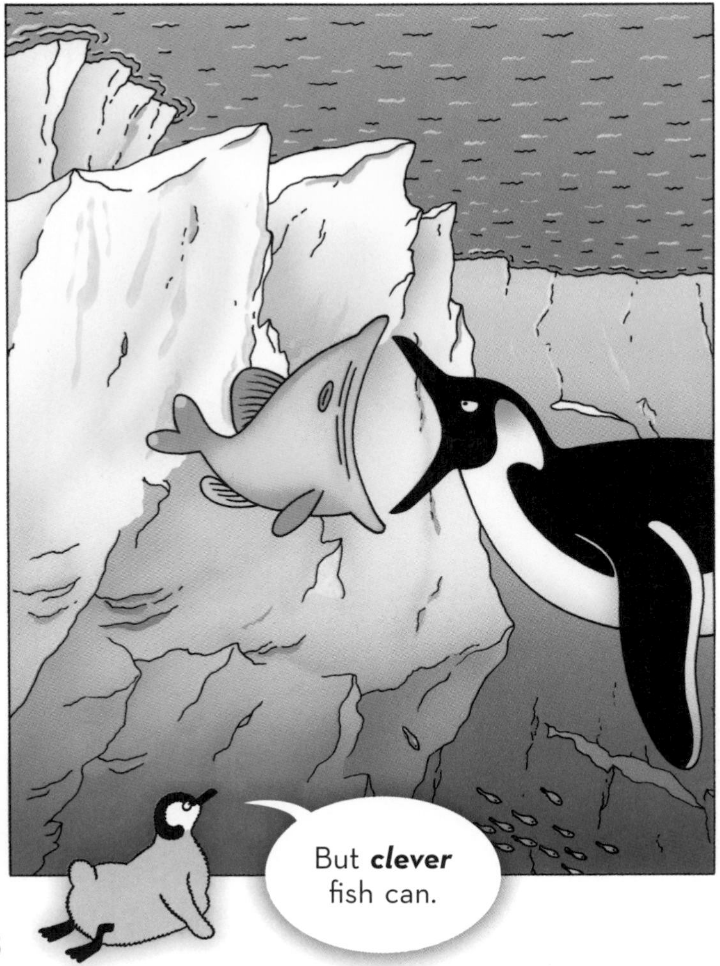
But **clever** fish can.

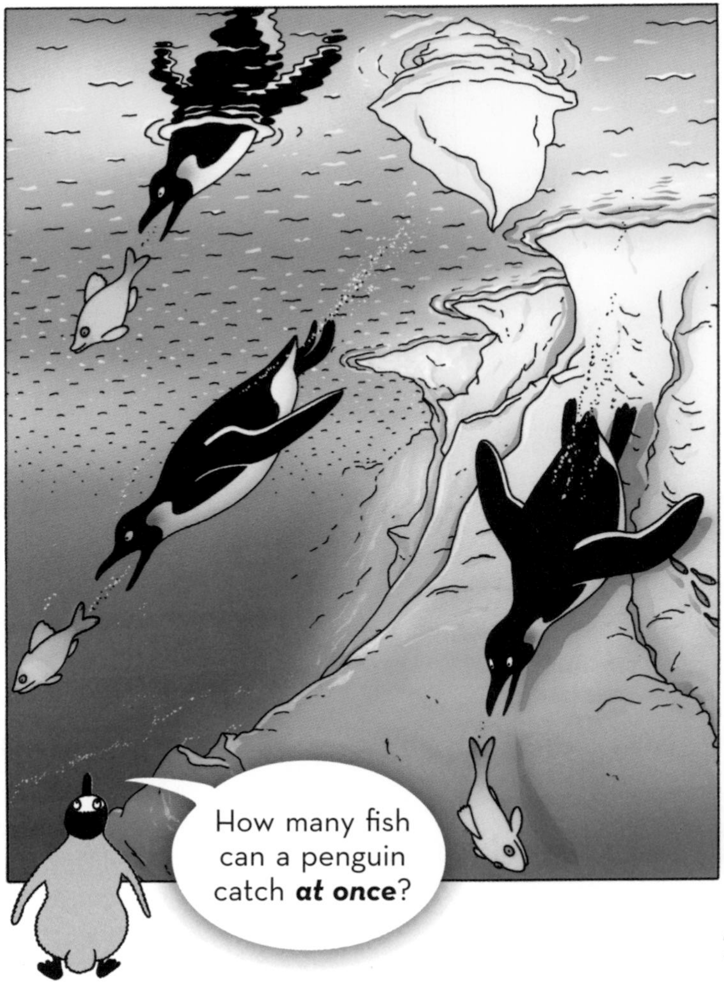
How many fish can a penguin catch **at once**?

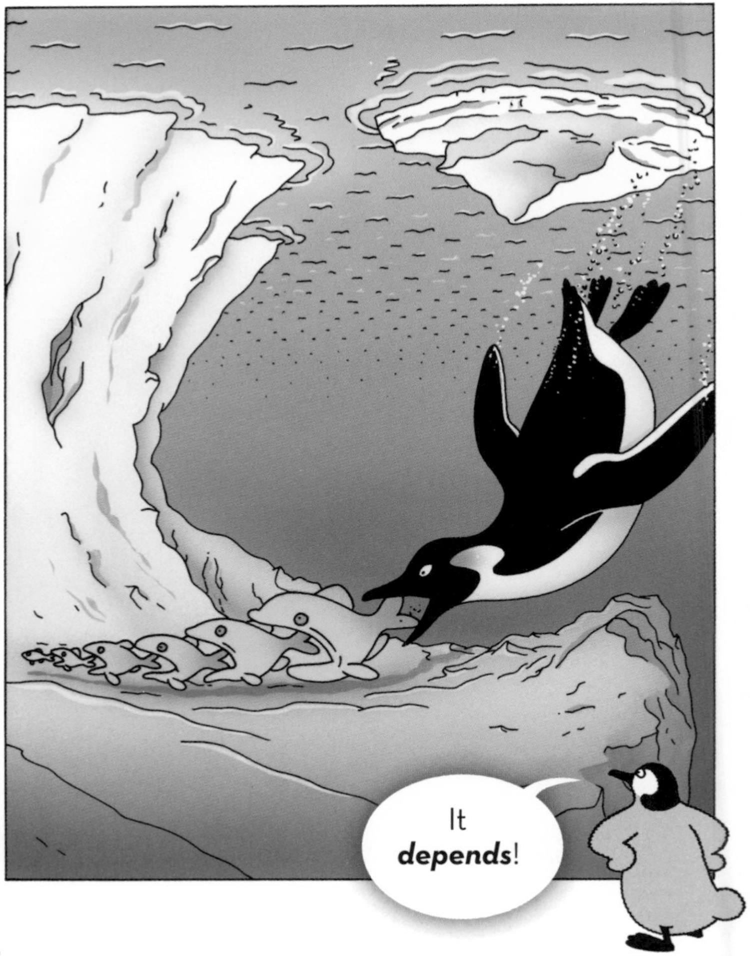
It **depends**!

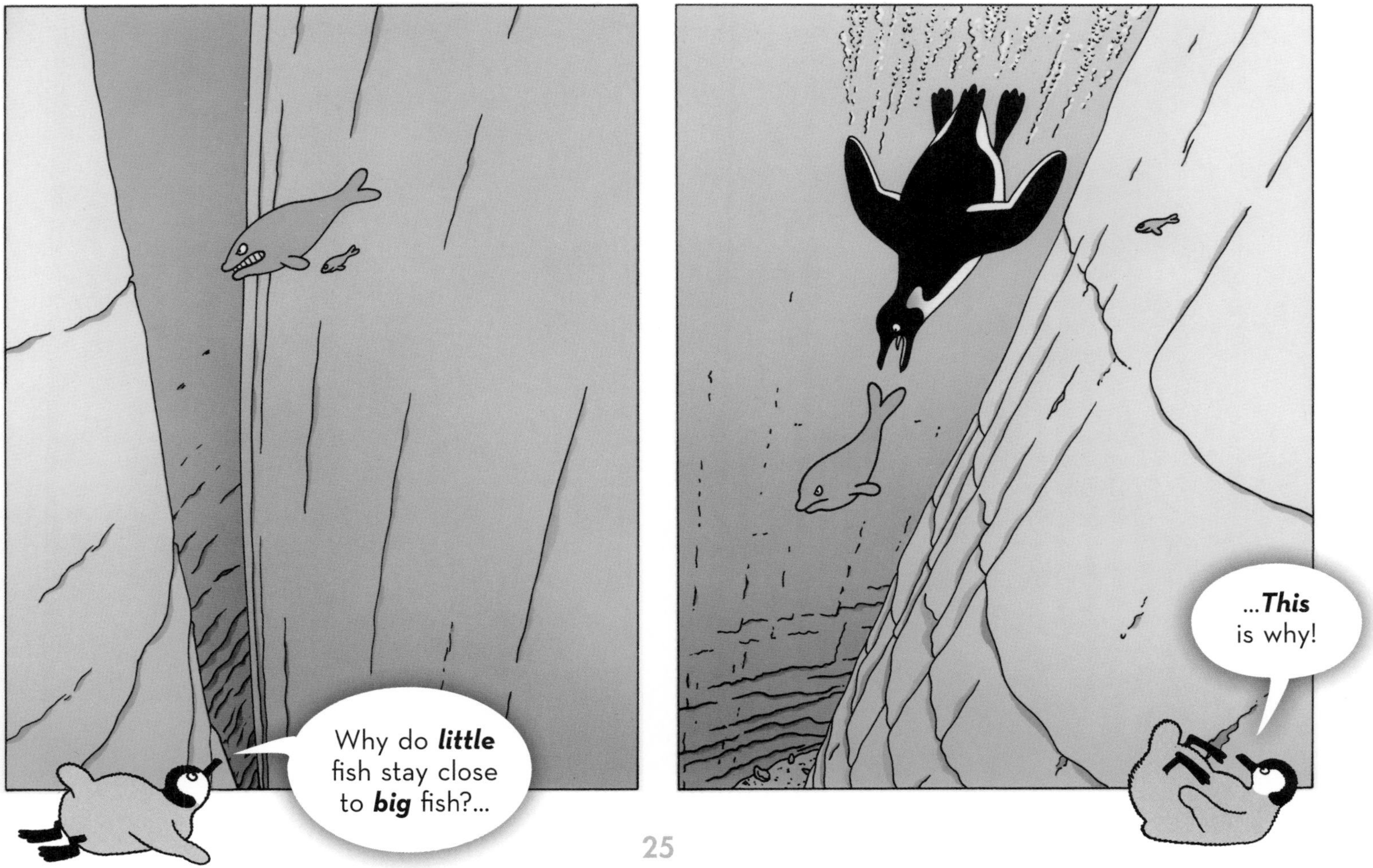
Why do little fish stay close to big fish?...
...This is why!

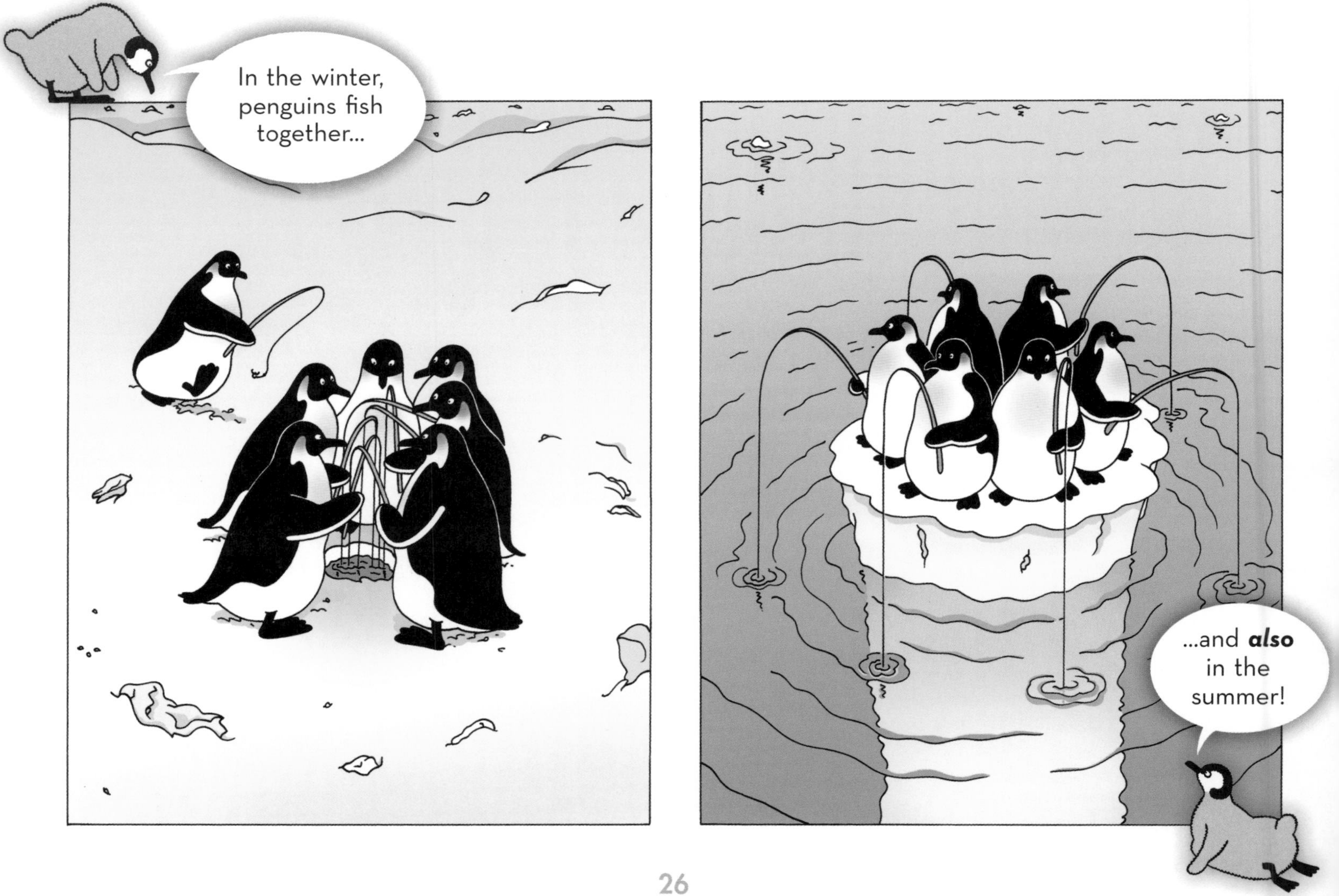
In the winter, penguins fish together...
...and **also** in the summer!

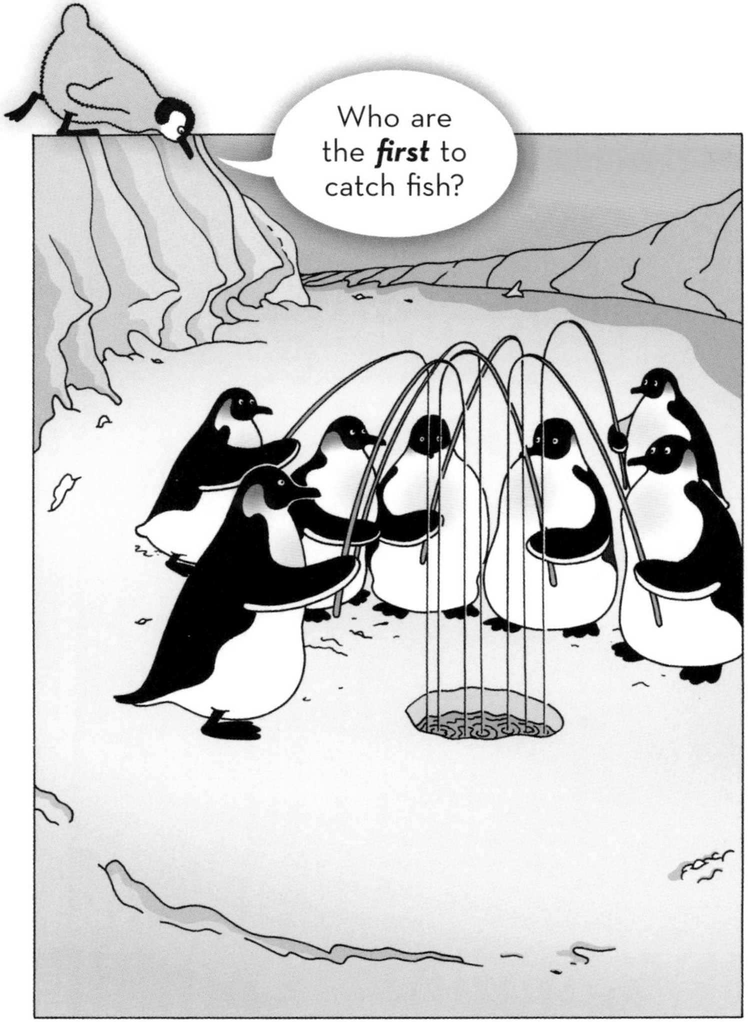
Who are the ***first*** to catch fish?

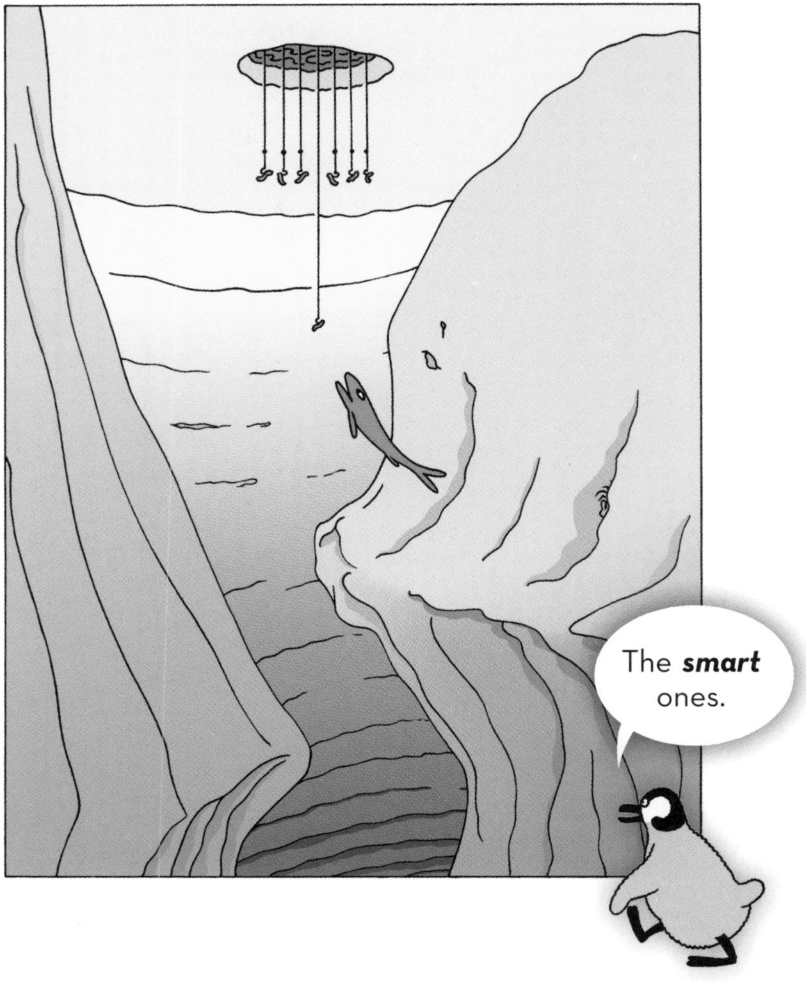
The ***smart*** ones.

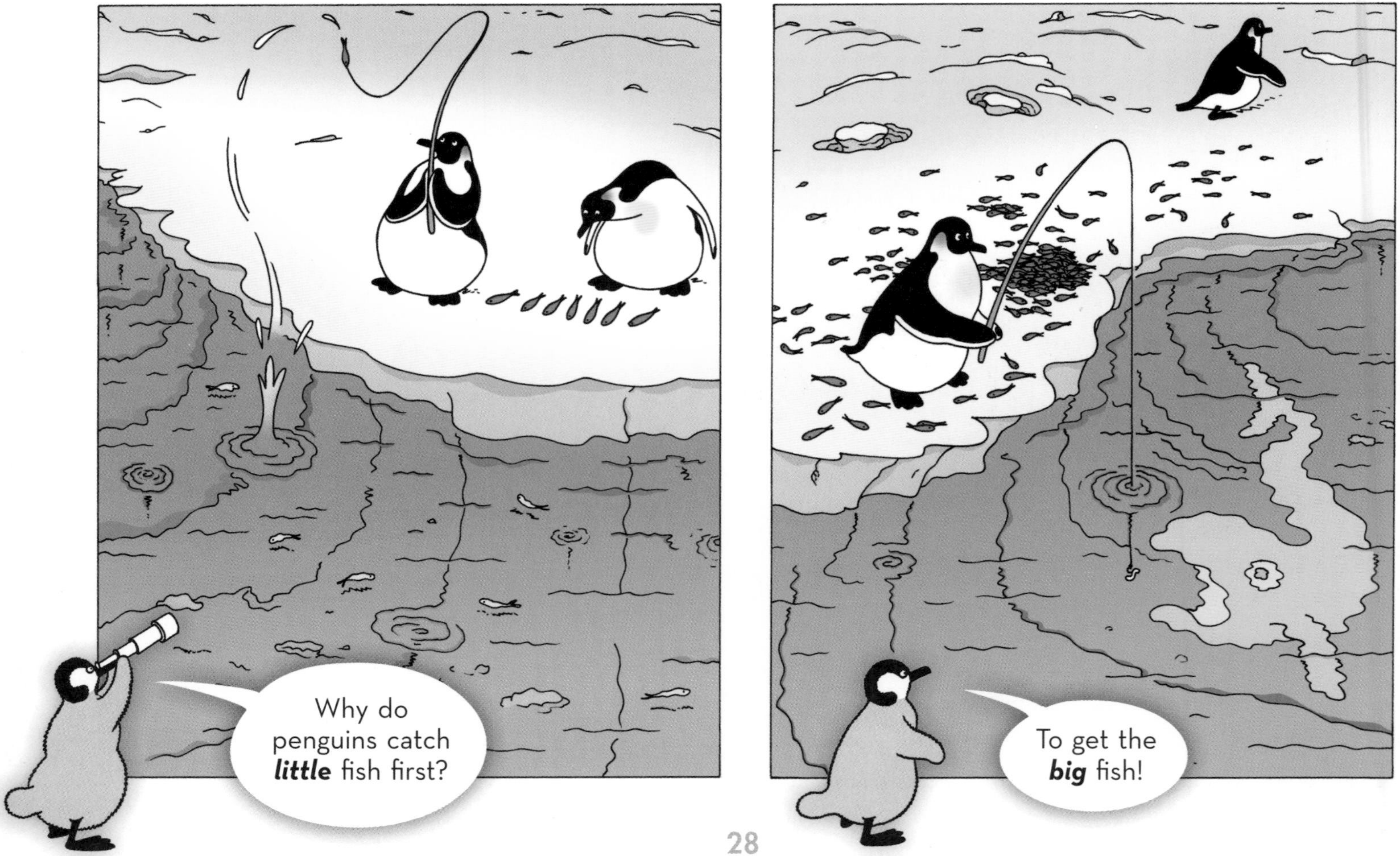
Why do penguins catch **little** fish first?
To get the **big** fish!

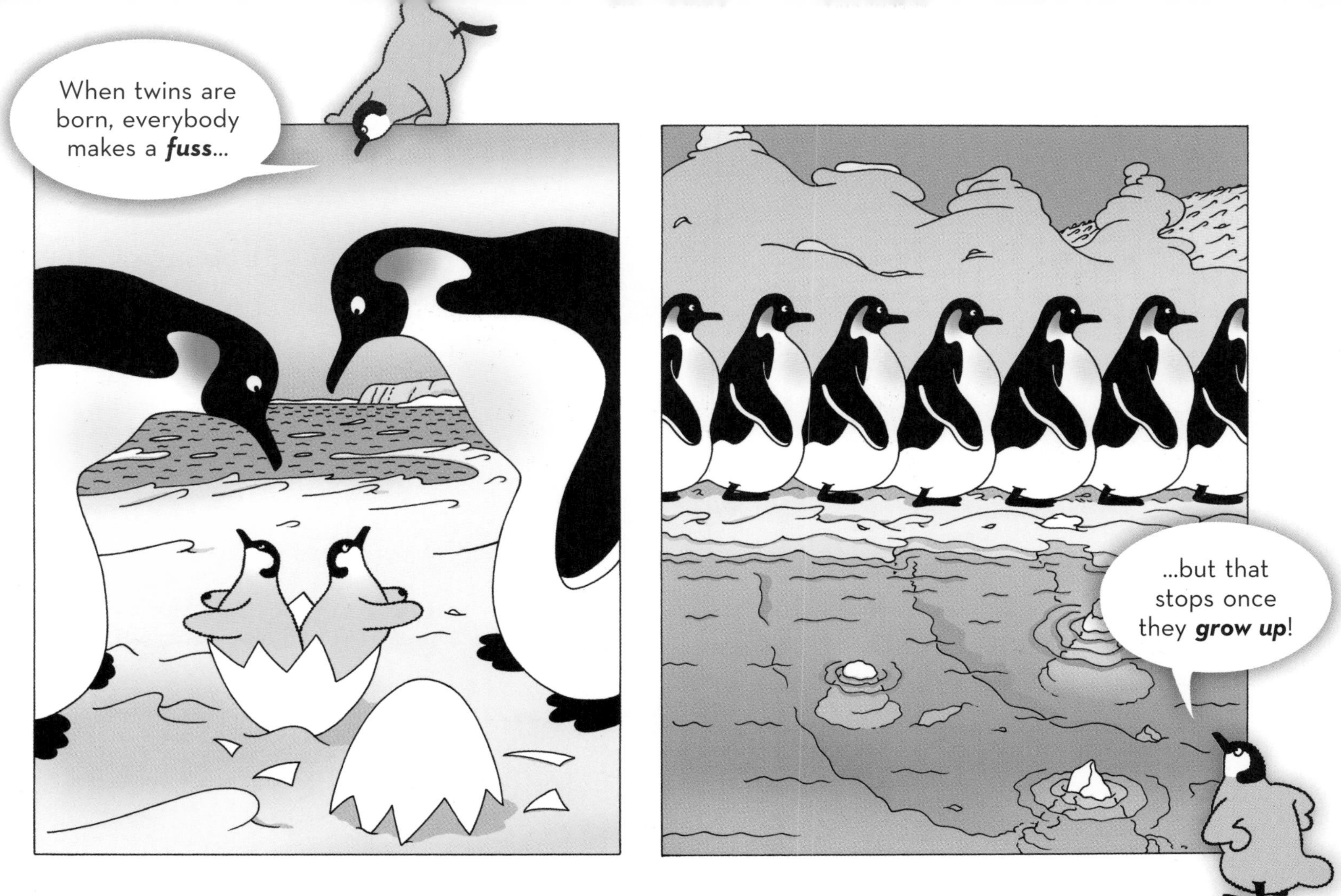
When twins are born, everybody makes a ***fuss***...
...but that stops once they ***grow up***!

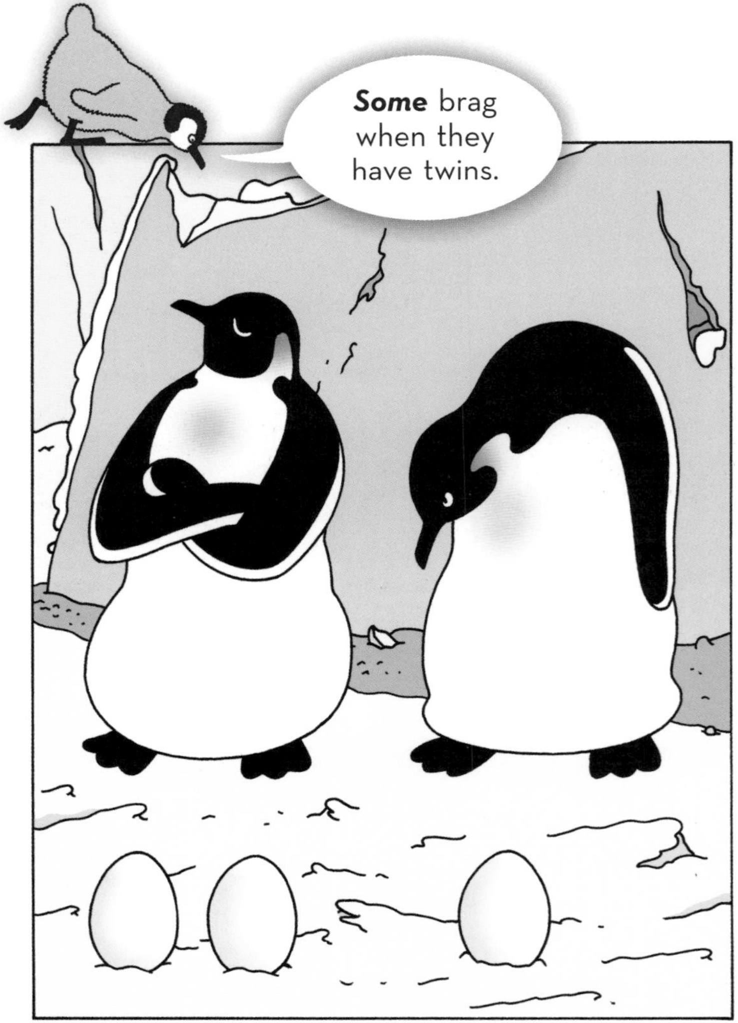
Some brag when they have twins.

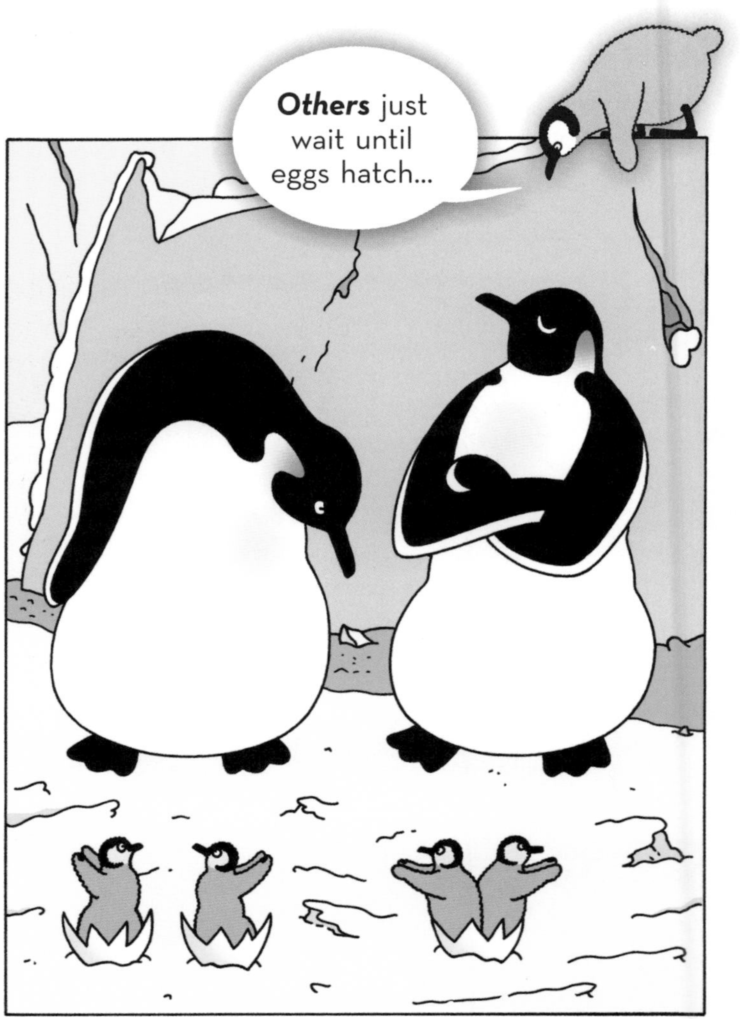
Others just wait until eggs hatch...

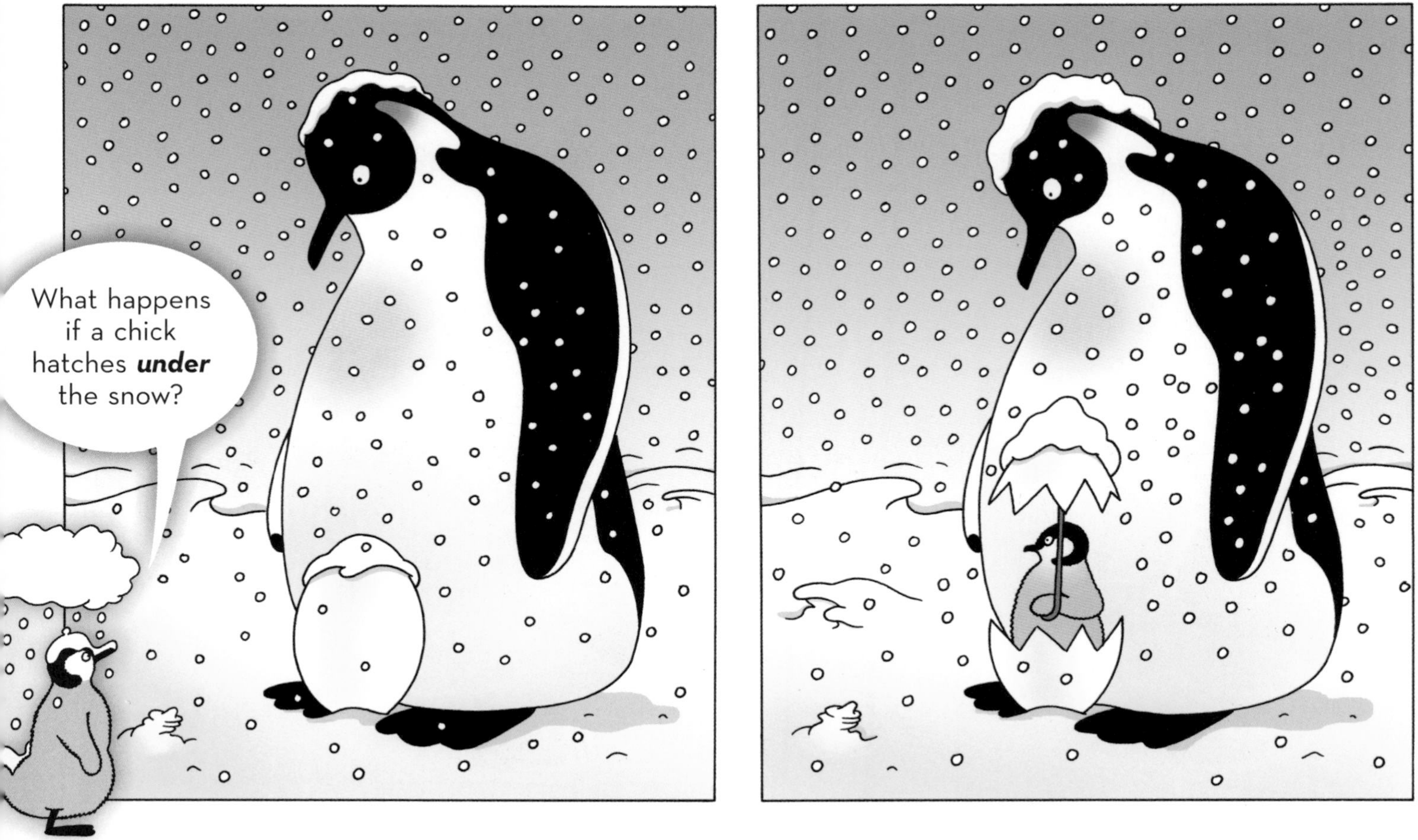
What happens if a chick hatches ***under*** the snow?

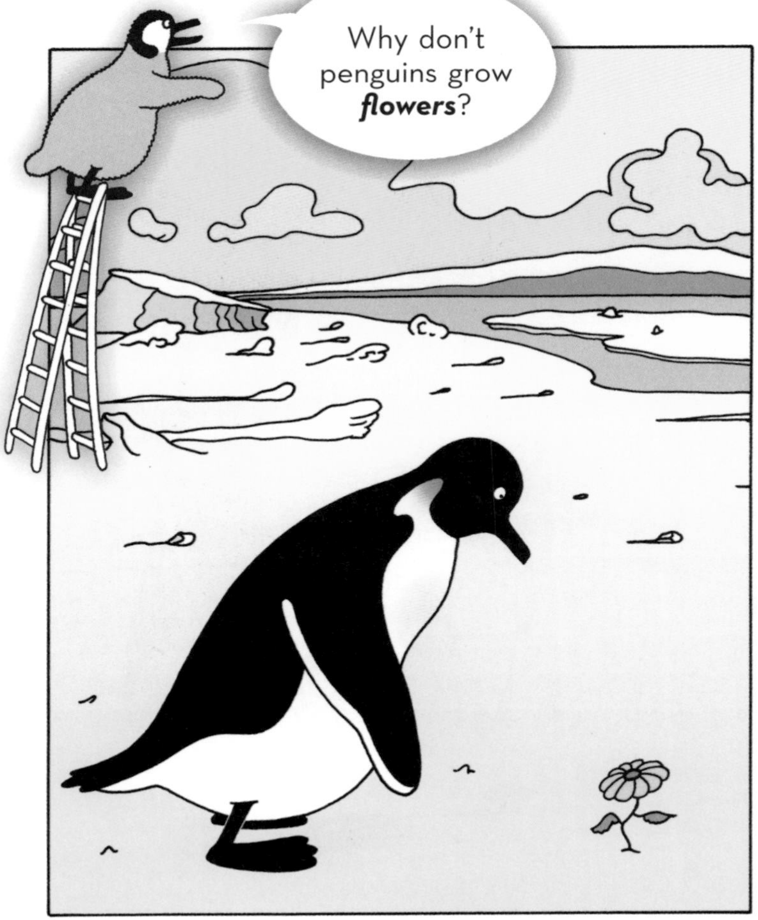
Why don't penguins grow **flowers**?

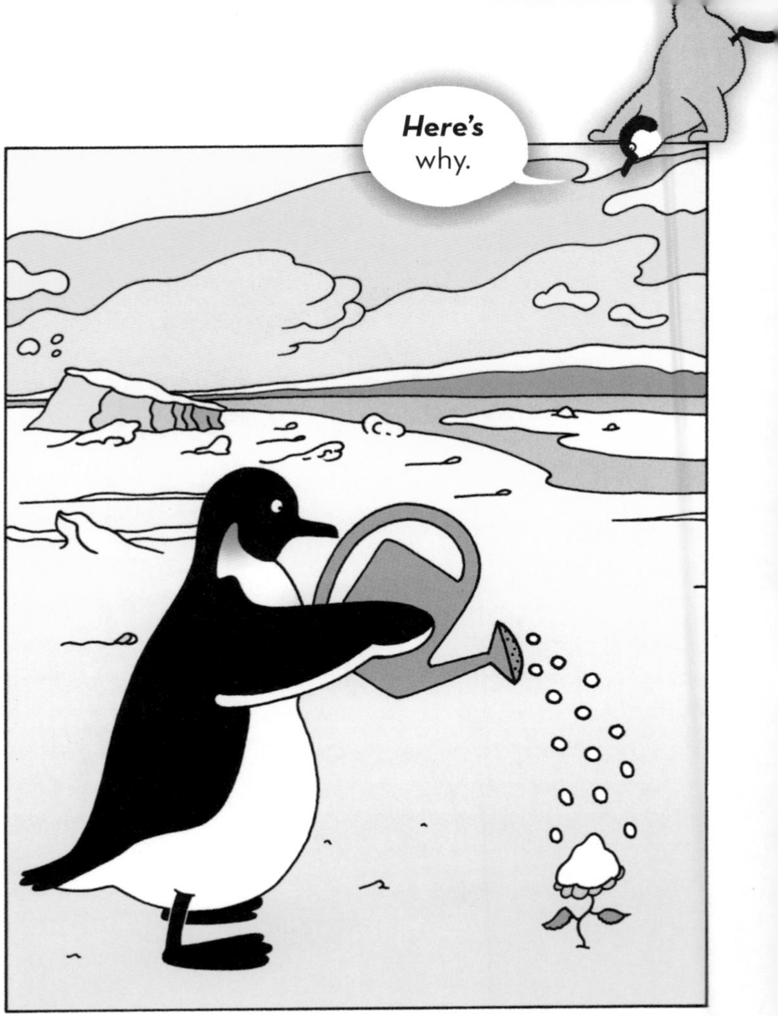
Here's why.

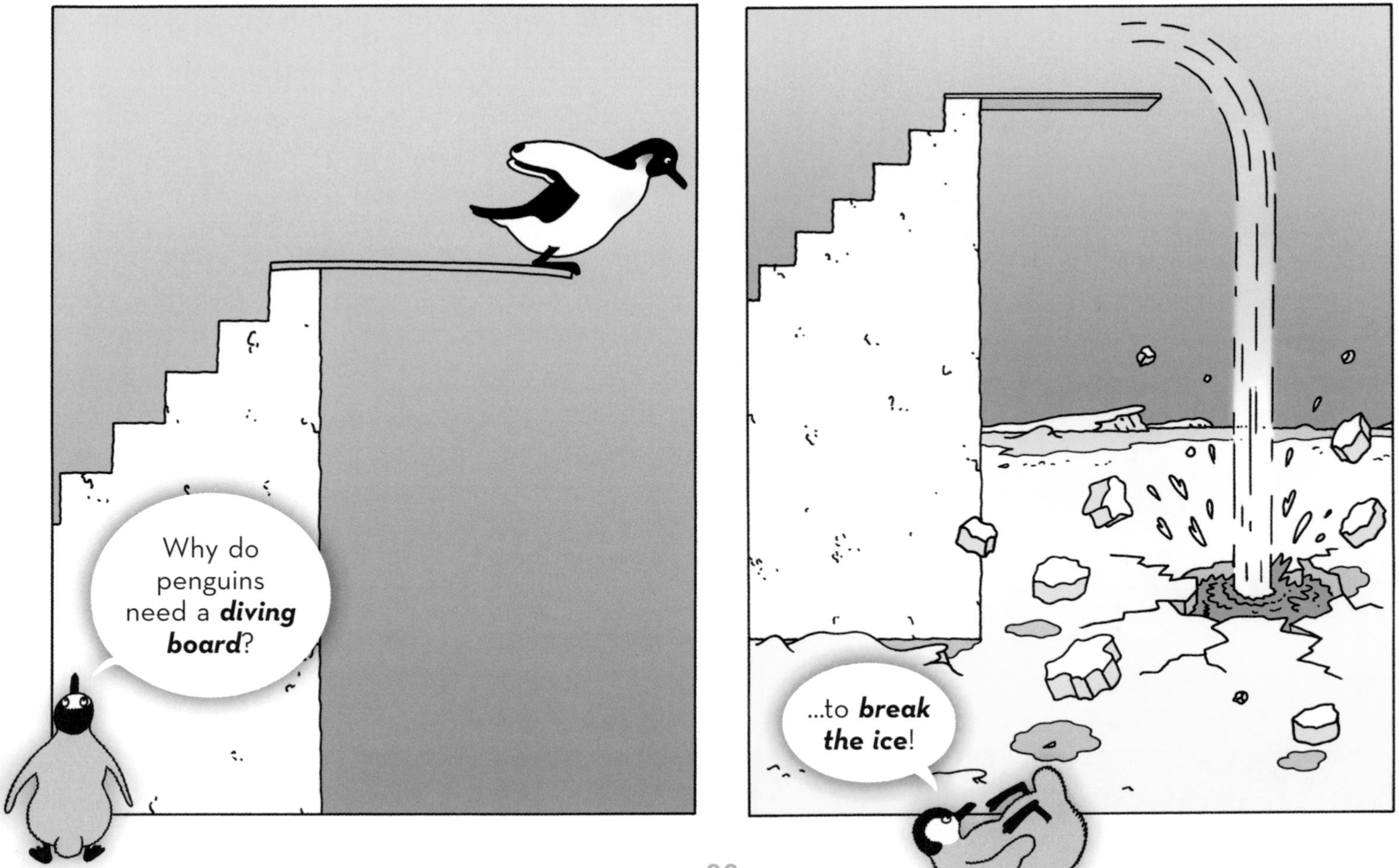
Why do penguins need a ***diving board***?
...to ***break the ice***!

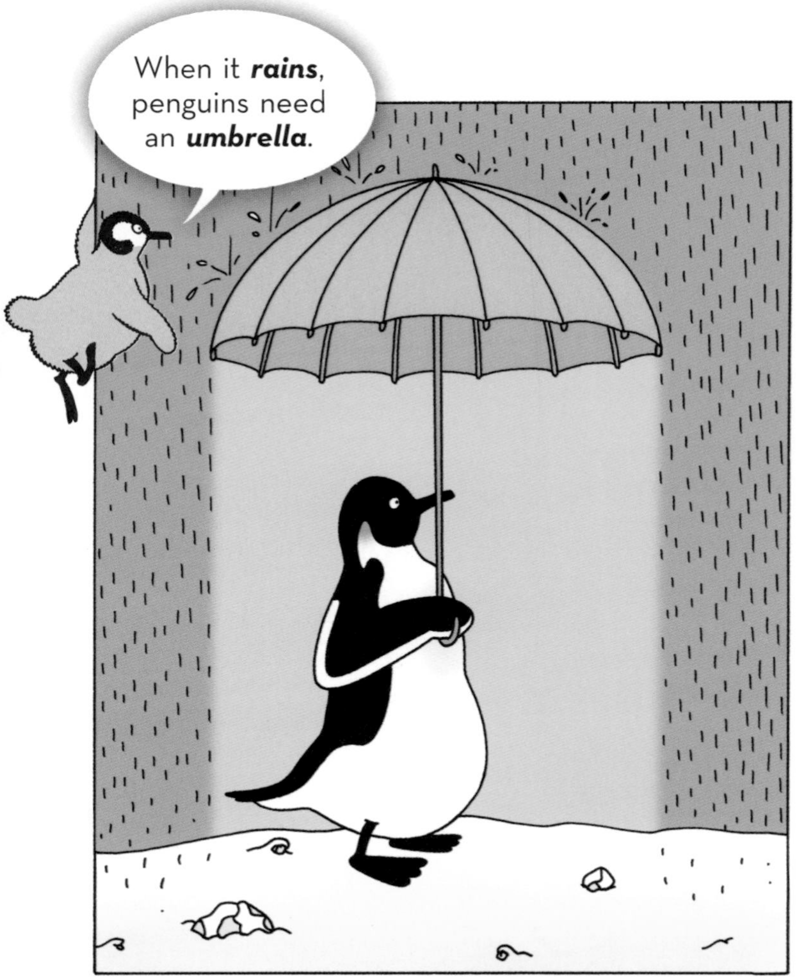
When it **rains**, penguins need an **umbrella**.

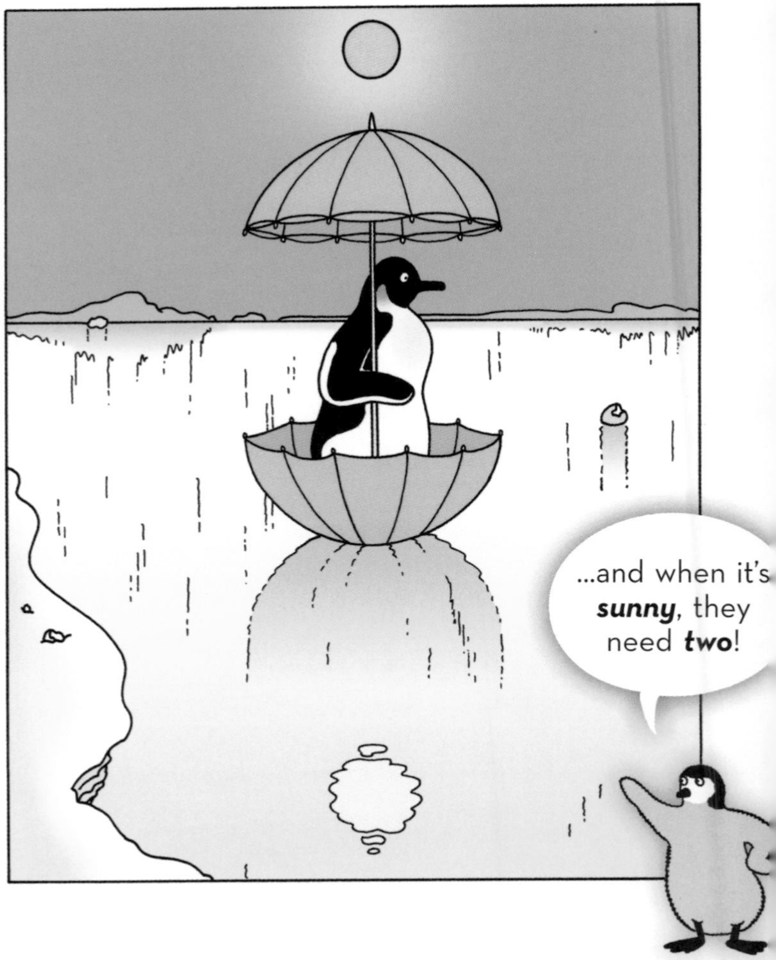
...and when it's **sunny**, they need **two**!

ABOUT THE AUTHORS

JEAN-LUC COUDRAY (who wrote this book) and **PHILIPPE COUDRAY** (who did the drawings) are twin brothers, both cartoonists in their native country of France. They identify with penguins in wanting people to tell them apart. Besides their respective comics, Jean-Luc also writes short stories and humorous novels, while Philippe enjoys painting in oil, making stereoscopic (3-D) images, and crypto-zoology—the study of undiscovered and mythical animals. Philippe's Benjamin Bear TOON books have received effusive praise and have been nominated twice for Eisner Awards. Both brothers enjoy nature, but while Jean-Luc enjoys hiking in Central France, the French forests aren't big enough for Philippe: he goes to the North American wilderness every year to search for Bigfoot.

And after all this goofiness...

AMAZING BUT TRUE: 100% GENUINE, REAL FACTS ABOUT PENGUINS!

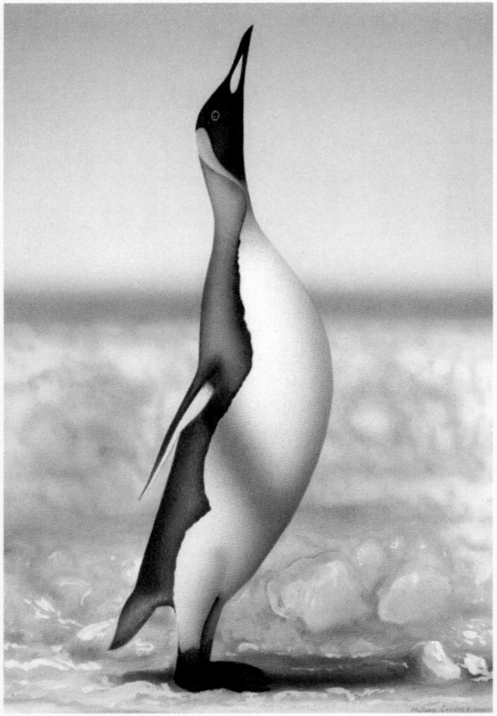

Emperor penguins, which are among the largest birds in the world, can grow to three or four feet tall.

Penguins are flightless birds. They spend most of their time on the ice and in the sea and live almost exclusively in the Southern Hemisphere, especially in Antarctica.

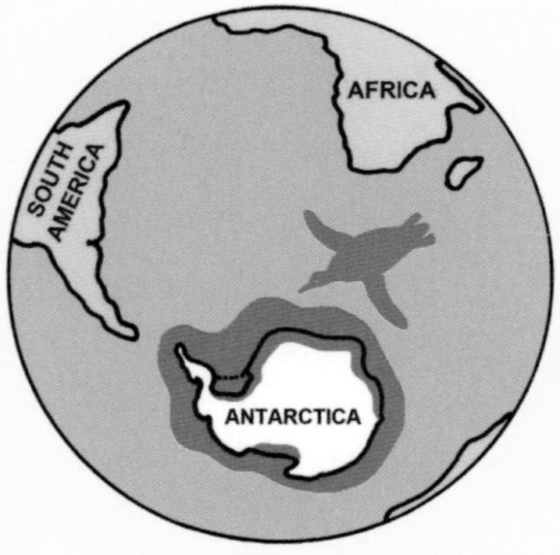
AFRICA
SOUTH AMERICA
ANTARCTICA

There are many kinds of penguins, such as the Adélie, Chinstrap, Gentoo, Rockhopper, Macaroni, and King penguins. This book focuses on Emperor penguins, the largest living species. Their closest relative is the King Penguin.

An adult penguin eats four to six pounds of food a day. Emperor penguins eat sea creatures, mostly krill and squid. Penguins dive for an average of three to six minutes, but the longest dive on record was twenty-two minutes. The deepest recorded dive was 1853 feet.

Emperor penguins mate during the deep Antarctic winter (which is our summer). They must face temperatures that can range from -4°F to -58°F,

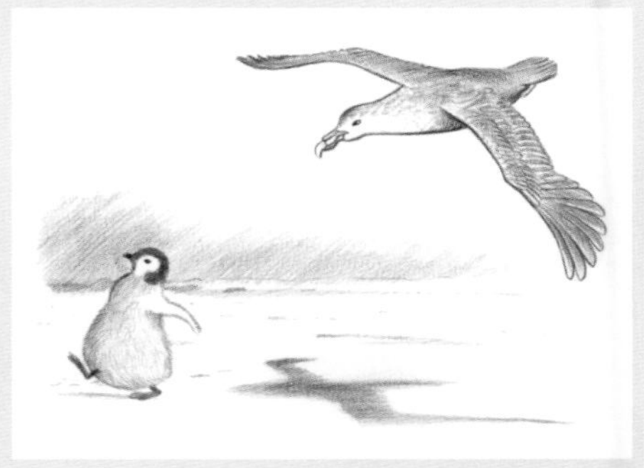

Giant petrels attack chicks.

ice and snow, and freezing winds up to 125 mph that blow off the polar plateau and intensify the cold. Feathers and a layer of body fat provide them with excellent insulation. They also have small bills and flippers, which conserves heat.

To fight the cold, about ten male penguins fit themselves into a tightly-packed huddle. The temperature inside the huddle can be as high as 74ºF. As penguins take turns moving from the cold outside to the warm inside, the huddle itself moves across the ice. Huddling means that Emperor penguins do not defend their territory, making them the only penguins that aren't territorial.

A male Emperor penguin sits on an egg to keep it

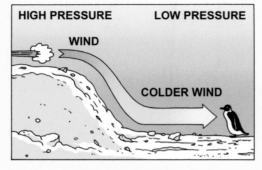

HIGH PRESSURE   LOW PRESSURE
WIND
COLDER WIND

warm for an average of sixty-four days. During this time, it eats no food and loses about forty percent of its body weight.

When it's time for the chicks to hatch, the females return from hunting with food for them. If the chicks hatch before then, the males spit up "milk," a secretion of protein and fat from their digestive tracts.

Leopard seals, orcas, and giant petrels are

Leopard seals are the greatest threat.

the penguins' main predators. If they're not eaten, penguins can live up to forty years, or even longer.

–Lydia Nguyen, TOON Educational Outreach

An orca is another predator.

FURTHER RESOURCES:

www.antarctica.gov.au/about-antarctica/wildlife/animals/penguins

lrs.ed.uiuc.edu/students/downey/project/penguins.html

www.penguins.cl/antarctic-penguins.htm

www.coolantarctica.com/Antarctica%20fact%20file/wildlife/Emperor-penguins.php

www.antarctica.ac.uk/about_antarctica/wildlife/birds/penguins/

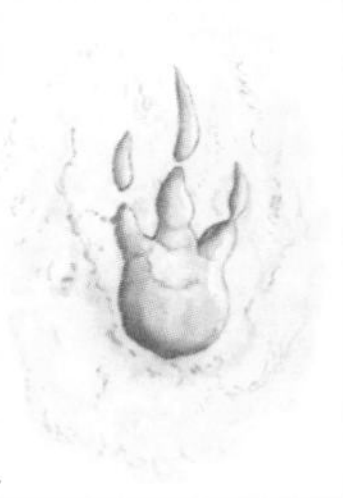

TIPS FOR PARENTS AND TEACHERS:

HOW TO READ COMICS WITH KIDS

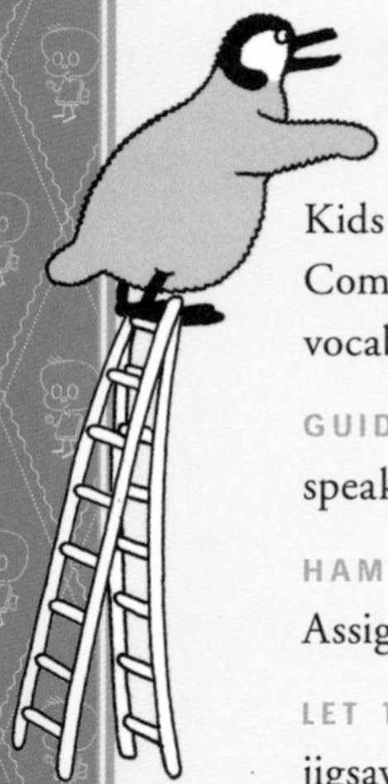

Kids love comics! They are naturally drawn to the details in the pictures, which make them want to read the words. Comics beg for repeated readings and let both emerging and reluctant readers enjoy complex stories with a rich vocabulary. But since comics have their own grammar, here are a few tips for reading them with kids:

GUIDE YOUNG READERS: Use your finger to show your place in the text, but keep it at the bottom of the speaking character so it doesn't hide the very important facial expressions.

HAM IT UP! Think of the comic book story as a play and don't hesitate to read with expression and intonation. Assign parts or get kids to supply the sound effects, a great way to reinforce phonics skills.

LET THEM GUESS. Comics provide lots of context for the words, so emerging readers can make informed guesses. Like jigsaw puzzles, comics ask readers to make connections, so check a young audience's understanding by asking "What's this character thinking?" (but don't be surprised if a kid finds some of the comics' subtle details faster than you).

TALK ABOUT THE PICTURES. Point out how the artist paces the story with pauses (silent panels) or speeded-up action (a burst of short panels). Discuss how the size and shape of the panels carry meaning.

ABOVE ALL, ENJOY! There is of course never one right way to read, so go for the shared pleasure. Once children make the story happen in their imagination, they have discovered the thrill of reading, and you won't be able to stop them. At that point, just go get them more books, and more comics.

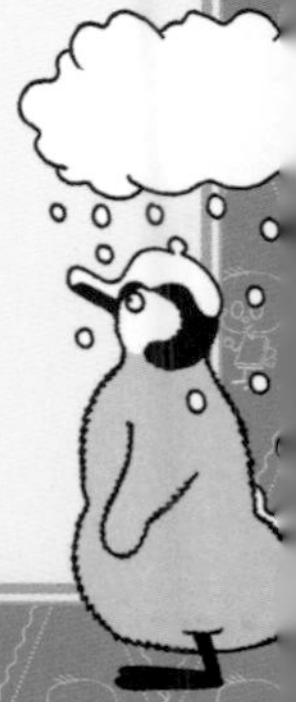